For
the Love
of a Life

For
the Love
of a Life

an unusual international love story

SIMON HOLDER

The Book Guild Ltd

First published in Great Britain in 2021 by
The Book Guild Ltd
9 Priory Business Park
Wistow Road, Kibworth
Leicestershire, LE8 0RX
Freephone: 0800 999 2982
www.bookguild.co.uk
Email: info@bookguild.co.uk
Twitter: @bookguild

This work is entirely fictitious and bears no resemblance to any persons living or dead.

Typeset in 11pt Minion Pro

Printed and bound by CPI Group (UK) Ltd, Croydon, CR0 4YY

ISBN 978 1913913 427

British Library Cataloguing in Publication Data.
A catalogue record for this book is available from the British Library.

Dear Reader: if you enjoyed this book, I would be hugely grateful if you would kindly leave a 4 or 5 star review on amazon.co.uk and/or bookguild.co.uk. Many thanks in anticipation.
Simon Holder.

Prologue

—〰—

Love is never, in its initial subjugation of the soul, what it appears to be; sometimes this disappointment is discovered in the protagonist, more usually in the affected. Yet neither party leaves without a scar, always deeper in one than the other. If not, there would always be a happy reconciliation.

This is what had happened to Xiao Feng.

She had always been beautiful, and knew it. She had always been intelligent, and knew that, too. She had been stylish from an early age, but that had been perfected by time. Her ability to attract men and nauseate women was partly natural but mostly contrived. It had meant she could pick, manipulate and acquire friendships, business contacts and potential lovers with ease, charmingly setting people against others and benefiting from the fragments they produced. Yet her apparent warmth and manufactured charm masked an inner emotional vacuum which she found difficult to fill; so despite her cleverness and acumen, these strengths clashed head-on when her first chance for true love presented itself.

That time, it was she who had been devastated in equal measure with the affected. She rued what she had done to her most loyal friend, who had continued to love her unconditionally. Perhaps stupidly. Yet she was angry that she continually wasted time fighting the admission without ever quite understanding it, always striving for the fiction that she was still in control, even when she knew she was not. She had had several chances to rectify the situation, but her stubborn refusal to admit that it was either reconcilable on the one hand, or her fault on the other, was testament to her resolute will, which would firmly deny the admission of any emotion presented to her.

Xiao Feng was born in Chengdu, China, the capital city of Sichuan, a central Chinese province of great beauty and much history. Her father was an academic who had at some time fallen foul of the Maoist dictatorship and been incarcerated for not espousing pure Communist views; her mother was a dentist who had been spared the indignity of prison because she was useful to the state and had been contrite in submission. Without any siblings, especially a brother, and with her father unavailable, the early male influence in her life was provided by her uncle on her father's side. Yet she soon found he was less a father figure than a predator, who forced her to stay in his company for long periods and made her reveal parts of her anatomy to him from an early age, which she initially agreed to without demur, not understanding the implications. After some years of this, her instinct, rather than her minimal worldly experience – which he restricted with a brutal will – sharpened her intellect in such a way as to make her realise the sinister side of his obsession. That something was unseemly became apparent to this beautiful child whilst still under the age of ten. Her mother was either unaware, too busy avoiding the shame of having a 'capitalist-roader' husband in prison, or was glad of the financial and emotional support her brother-in-law provided and so turned a blind eye. Yet to the suddenly aware Xiao Feng, she was cognisant that her mother had betrayed her, and it was the first of many scars to affect her young life.

Her uncle had forbidden her to mention anything at school, whether to her few friends or the teachers, and would always take her there in the mornings and meet her in the afternoons, at both times giving her a stern look and a finger to his lips, denoting silence. It was an image that persisted in her mind forever and which, in later life, would give her nightmares whenever his stern, admonishing face crossed her subconscious. She was a prisoner. Yet she got used to it, as it seemed normal; after all, she knew little else, and as he had also instructed her to work hard at school and would brook no slacking, there was little time to understand his motives. Or, thus, to question them.

One day, just after her tenth birthday, her mother went away to visit Xiao Feng's father, her husband, in prison, which was far away in Beijing. She would be absent for five days, four of which would be spent travelling there and back, and Xiao Feng dreaded being alone without her. Not that her mother restrained her uncle: it was just that she was there and by being so had a restricting influence on him. For the first time, Xiao Feng had locked the bathroom door when she went in to wash, and for the first time too he banged on the door and shouted to let him in. She was pleased with her suddenly found defiance, but this acted as a catalyst when she left for her tiny room, for he was already there waiting for her, and when she entered he locked the door behind her and put the key out of reach. Then he raped her, her screams unheard in the brutal concrete of the state-constructed tenement.

This happened every night until her mother returned, but his expression was the one he always gave her at school, his menace so palpable and omnipresent that she would never dare tell her mother anyway.

It was the same from then on, whenever her mother went out, or was at work, or visited friends or her father. Once, she pleaded to be able to go with her to see him, not just because she had forgotten what her father looked like, but to get away – just to get away – and to have her father cuddle her like he used to do and laugh with her. There was never any laughter now. In years to come, she would realise that her mother had always known of her uncle's abuse of her, but he was high up in the government and was not only influential and well paid but could have accused her mother of complicity with her husband's crimes: so she had kept quiet, silent and submissive.

If there was one good thing to come out of this period, it was that Xiao Feng became a superb runner, and excelled at it; she needed to be. As she became ever more beautiful as a young woman, she wanted one day to be able to run from her uncle and also any potential assailants. She honed her intellect, too, and was always top of the class in every subject; yet this made her classmates envious and wary of her, so she had little solace at school either, and studying and running were her only escape.

Not long before she finished at school, her father returned home, his prison sentence abbreviated for good behaviour – and also because Mao had died in 1976 and now, a few years after, a slight liberalism had permeated China under Deng Xiaoping. Her uncle suddenly just disappeared, but if she did ever see him again she ran as fast as she could away from him – in any direction, anywhere – much to the bemusement of her father, who knew nothing. She had by now just won a place at university, which meant going to Beijing, and would also never need to go home again: the terrors were too deep. And if she did well, she could see her father when she wanted to and probably avoid her mother.

She did well at university and her father did, indeed, visit her there from time to time; as an academic and re-instated teacher, his brain had recovered from its prison-induced torpor and he had become even sharper and more perceptive than before: as a result, he had sensed that something terrible had invaded his beautiful daughter's soul, and although he wanted to know what it was, he feared he might also be afraid to hear it. So he said nothing. And that was how it stayed, for, after a meeting in Beijing, he had returned to Chengdu and suddenly died. Yet her mother did not bother to tell her: Xiao Feng found out a year later from a lady, an old family friend, who came to see her in Beijing. She never forgave her mother for this and still missed her father deeply, who had been the only solace she had had in her early years. Yet at least now that she was away from her uncle's abuse and clutches, she could blossom, and not only did she do ever better at her studies but also began to make tentative friends and start a meagre social life which had so cruelly been denied her before.

As if to confirm a new outlook, and a new her, she decided to do what many Chinese girls do – give herself a Western name. She felt this would help her burgeoning global ambitions and make her stand out – and her new name would be better remembered by the Western companies she could now hope to work for. She found one in a magazine which she felt suited her – Berenice. It sounded worldly, unusual, upmarket and pretty – just like her. This change gave her an added confidence, as if she was shaking off the past and becoming a new woman – even if she still retained the same fears and sufferings. So as she blossomed intellectually, she bloomed physically, too, and was not short of advances from many young men: it was hardly surprising, as she had become a stunningly beautiful young woman, her olive skin, butterfly lips and slim physique a magnet for anyone who appreciated beauty. But her traumas had terrified her, so she resisted all advances, becoming known as a frigid woman who did not know what was good for her.

Yet she knew all too well…

Chapter One

—⦿—

Berenice had persisted with her love of running at university, her resolution to keep fit a dark, brooding necessity at the back of her mind, and at times it was very useful. On a number of occasions she had been on a bus or train and received unwelcome attentions from not only the more loutish sort of men but even those in suits who were well-groomed. Perhaps her sense of fashion helped: now aware that she had been a sex object when a child, she nonetheless instinctively wanted to do all she could to retain her beauty for as long as she was able, for she knew it was power. Knowing also that it was transient, she had acquired a stylish mode of dressing well but cheaply, which she had gleaned from the Italian magazines that had become available in her once-closed country. She had perused them with fervour because, although she outwardly resisted men's advances, she was very aware she wanted to like male company and did, indeed, find some of these men attractive. Yet the terrors remained, and she wanted to be loved for herself, not her looks. The thought of sex again was a hurdle that she knew would have to be surmounted one day – not just because she eventually wanted children but because she felt it might just be pleasurable under the right circumstances. Yet by having had intercourse forced upon her it never had been, and so if that situation had happened again in a supposedly benign relationship she was fearful of disdaining and avoiding it forever. The magazines, though, gave her the confidence and chutzpah to carry off the whistles and comments without demeaning herself, and her fashion sense would mean she could still be attractive long after the bloom of youth had deserted her.

Being stylish would have other benefits, too: when she went for job interviews she could arrest the male questioners with one look and have them in the palm of her hand for the rest of the event; that way, she got the best offers for the best jobs at the best firms. She turned them all down until, one day, she met someone who would change her life forever but, this time, it would be joyful. For a time, at least.

Arriving at a huge international fashion firm which had started recruiting in China, she was greeted by a pleasant man of a few years older than she who was slightly shy and therefore had an unthreatening air about him. He was also witty and charming, and came from a part of China she did not know, which made him slightly mysterious, his slightly craggy looks being less prevalent in Beijing. He was not quite well-dressed, despite his position and the company he worked for, but he had a presence and a turn of phrase she found engaging. He stayed in the room as she was interviewed by a fat American man whose drawl he interpreted when necessary. Yet she had understood most of what he said anyway, having studied English hard when at school and then continuing to hone it when at university; intuitively, she had somehow felt it would be useful one day – and even another means of escape. The man offered her a job on the spot, and she found herself accepting. The money was good, the perks were better... and she could not help but like this young man who had shown her in. In fact, she asked for his personal phone number, which surprised her as much as it embarrassed him; but he complied and she gave him hers.

On her way out, she turned to see him looking after her with what looked like a loving incomprehension in his eyes, and he gave a feeble wave as the revolving doors swirled between their respective gazes. They met up a week later.

The boy's name – for compared to her, he *was* a boy – was Shuo. He was not yet quite a man, in her view, and she had acquired a womanly perspective on life which gave her, if not quite an air of superiority, a worldly demeanour, augmented by her style and looks; she realised she was educated and knowledgeable compared to most others, and she enjoyed sounding superior without being patronising or haughty. It was a clever way of keeping Shuo on his toes and her in the ascendant. It worked perfectly. One thing that she did love about him, which she could not do, was write poetry, which he did profusely for her. It was not that good, but being bespoke for her made it better, and she enjoyed coming home in the evenings and finding he had been to her flat and pushed one under the door. Sex had not reared its head yet, for which she was grateful. He was too timid and still in awe of this learned, worldly beauty who, for some reason, seemed to like him –which surprised, excited and terrified him in equal measure. For her, this slow burn was just what she needed – she wanted to be sure, to be ready, to be in charge and seize the moment when it occurred. Which she knew it would, as she was controlling things.

The day job was easy for her; she was in touch with suppliers of clothes across China and its neighbouring countries, and her easy, articulate and engaging personality made her popular and instantly memorable to the majority of people she came into contact with. And when she met them face to face, they remembered her even more. She had an eye for style and quality when searching out new lines, too: she also made astute recommendations to businesses as to how to improve their designs, so helping them and her company; she was soon seen as someone who managed to get the best balance between quality and price, lending the odd inspired touch to a garment which made it not just attractive but exceptional. Her stock began to rise, and with it her ambition.

Chapter Two

—⁓—

During this time, she and Shuo had become ever closer, yet he was inevitably wondering whether Berenice really liked him or just enjoyed having good-looking male company to impress her business colleagues – she had no real friends as far as he could see. His doubts were underlined by the fact that sex had not 'happened' yet, and he started to wonder whether it ever would. It frequently seemed to be about to, but his innate shyness – and not wanting to risk what he already had with her – meant he never pushed his advantage at the relevant moment. She would then get up and start to work again. So he stopped sending her poems and became a little distant, but was upset when she did not seem to notice. One day, out of growing frustration, he confronted her about it. They were lounging in her flat, and she was, as usual, busy on her laptop, so he used the premise that surely she did not need to work over this weekend, especially as she was doing so well in her job already that it seemed unnecessary. At least to him.

She put the laptop down and looked at him with her beautiful brown eyes, the slight breeze from the open balcony doors ruffling her short but slightly wavy russet-black hair, and making the outline of her small, pert breasts visible through her white T-shirt.

"Dear Shuo," she said. "I want to be successful. Therefore, I have to work hard. If you think I'm going to stay in this company forever, you're wrong. I have ambition, and I cannot stop until I have achieved great things."

"I have a great ambition, too," he said simply. "I want to love you. We've been going out a few weeks now and—"

"I know you love me, Shuo, but I have to be focussed. If I were to fall in love with you it would divert me from my motivation. I will not allow that."

"OK. Then I'm going home."

"OK. See you tomorrow at work." And she went back to her laptop.

Shuo stood for a moment in disbelief at her offhand comment then realised it was over and picked up the few things he had been allowed to leave in her flat. Then he left. He was upset, sad and angry. Frustrated, too. To him, the most beautiful girl he had ever met had just rebuffed him as if he was irrelevant, in the way, unimportant. Yet they had had some wonderful times together, made many mutual friends, been to some inspiring places together. Was she just a companion to him in her eyes? They had come so close to making love, too, on so many occasions, his emotions bursting with desire for her and she, apparently, for him. Yet it never actually happened. Was there some deep secret in her soul which made her afraid of sex, or commitment, or letting go?

Arriving outside, it had started to rain, so he travelled the short distance home on the bus, the crowded streets of Beijing such a blur to him that he nearly missed his stop. As he opened the door of his empty, lonely, unkempt flat – in such contrast to the studied, stylish neatness of hers, where everything was there just because it had its place – its desolation only contributed to his over-riding feeling of total confusion.

An hour or so after he had gone, Berenice finished her research and typing up a report, then looked around. Where was Shuo? He hadn't really gone, had he? She had been so engrossed in her work that she had not really taken heed of anything. She called for him and looked in the bedroom, expecting to find him lurking in the corner, with that look of studied disappointment which she had become so used to. Silly boy! She would have to admonish him at work tomorrow. She made herself a drink of tea then suddenly realised she wanted him there now, needed his presence, to make her feel whole again – and a desired woman in every sense.

She called him on his mobile but there was no response, just the usual annoying voicemail message. So she went to the phone in her hallway and rang his home number. No answer. Perhaps he was not back in his flat yet. She would wait. She would try again, though: she wanted him here with her. Yet, as with so many times before, a vision of her uncle raping her came back: she knew she wanted Shuo to make love with her but was terrified of it either going so horribly wrong that she might lose him, or being so wonderful that it would distract her. Also, if she capitulated and took away the promise of sex with him, she might not be able to control him any more, and that could be a huge loss. Would he still be putty in her hands if she gave in?

She tried his number again. Nothing. She decided to go for a walk... might even turn up at his flat with fake tears to show her contrition. Then things could go back to normal. After all, she did not want people at work to think that she had been dumped by someone so uninfluential as Shuo. That would do nothing for her image of robust professionalism and control. She put on her outside shoes and, seeing it had been raining, picked up an umbrella which matched them, and left.

In his flat, Shuo had seen his mobile ring and ignored it; and after it had gone to voicemail, he blocked her number. Then he watched the landline phone as it rang – twice – and again resisted the temptation to answer it. If it was her, he was going to play hard to get – his friends had told him that often worked. And if it wasn't her, it didn't matter anyway. He looked outside and saw the rain had stopped, giving way to a transient sunshine, so he decided to go out: his flat was claustrophobic and stuffy. Which was another reason he had always preferred being at hers...

There was a small open space on the way between each of their flats, wedged between the expressionless slabs of high-rise housing. It was not exactly a park but a turgid piece of worn grass with a few seats and a small man-made pond which had been included in the development as a nod to nature, which was akin to putting rouge on a corpse to Berenice; but they had often gone there to feed the ducks which had somehow appeared – despite being in acute danger in Beijing – or to sit on one of the seats with a picnic.

Shuo found himself heading for the bench they normally sat on, not to wallow in what might have been but rather to lay a ghost if this really was the end, as it seemed to be. There were other girls in the office and several had made it quite obvious they liked him, so he felt there would be no problem finding another. Yet none of them were like Berenice. She had style, ambition, presence... although he often wondered whether she really was too good for him. He always tried to banish that thought because it was cowardly: no, of course he was as good as she was; he was just a slow starter, like most boys. Boy? No, he was a young man. Then his diffidence returned: no, he was still a boy, whereas Berenice, despite being a little younger than him, was already a woman. Yes, she was too good for him. He sighed. Well, as from tomorrow, he would work much harder, ignore her and show her that he could start to achieve like she already had. That would make her respect him again, and then he could rub in the snub by going off with one of the others. That would show her.

His eyes focussed on the other side of the tiny, dirty pond... There was a pretty girl there, and he felt immediately drawn to her, as if his vision had been guided by an unseen force to notice her. And she was just staring at him, with a smile on her face, waiting for him to perceive her. He blinked. She waved. But it was not Berenice. He stood up and intimated that they should meet by the end of the tiny stretch of water. She coyly agreed, and a few moments later they were facing one another. They nervously exchanged some pleasantries and, finding themselves next to a food vendor, bought some dumplings and sat down on the bench Shuo had vacated a minute or two before. Her name was

Lin Yang, and she was even prettier than he had initially realised.

At the moment they sat down, with their backs to the food-seller and staring at the pond – if not yet too often at each other – Berenice walked past, en route for Shuo's flat. She was thinking too deeply to notice them, her eyes focussed on the ground as she contemplated her best strategy to defuse the situation which had just been presented to her. She did not want to lose Shuo but wished the relationship to develop on her terms, not his. She was the dominant person in this partnership and she would have the last word. If he waited for her to get over her inner barriers, she mused, then she would not hold back on allowing him to experience the inevitable pleasures of her body. They got on well: yes, he was not nearly as bright as she was, but he had a good heart, and he could be moulded and manipulated into exactly what she wanted. Her realisation that he was very sexual had been obvious from the start and this was why she had proceeded with caution: yes, that's what she would tell him. It would eventually work beautifully for them both. Perhaps she might even be able to offer herself this time to him… well, if she could use the situation to quell her reservations. That was the sticking-point, though: she had no idea how a man touching her again after all this time would affect her emotions. But she would have to be strong, and she prided herself in being just that, so she would prevail whichever way the encounter went.

She arrived at Shuo's flat and rang the buzzer. Nothing. She rang again. Nothing once more. A spurt of anger shot up her body: she knew he was there – he never left his flat except to see her or go to work, like most boys: they played games on their laptops and looked at porn or watched films. He was definitely there. When, after a few minutes of more insistent buzzing she began to realise he probably was not – he would never have been able to resist her for that long – she felt angry and disappointed. He must have predicted that she would come to him and that annoyed her – she had been second-guessed and she did not like it.

Despondently and with her sense of purpose thwarted, Berenice mooched back in the direction of her flat, only stopping to buy a drink at the food-seller in the open space. Twilight was enveloping the previously sunny afternoon and even the ducks were quiet in anticipation of a cold night on their little fetid pond. Suddenly, a chill went through her body – although she was unsure whether it was due to the cold or a reaction to how she had just lost control for the first time in her life since she'd left home and the clutches of her uncle. Whichever the reason, she now felt somewhat uncomfortable about the situation she was in...

—ɯ—

In Lin Yang's tiny flat, Shuo was doing his best to act responsibly and demurely. She was a good communicator and much more open than Berenice, with a propensity for small talk which both delighted and quietened him, as he could not easily get a word in edgeways. She was not as intelligent as Berenice, nor as stylish, but he could change that over time. Her clothes were cheap and did not match, unlike the girl he instinctively felt he should be with. Yet Yang was available, open and wanted to know him in the most intimate way possible, it seemed, and his intent was suddenly to explore her as much as he could, almost as a riposte to the restraint visited upon him by Berenice. There was one thing he already did not like about Lin – he noticed she had a tattoo on her otherwise beautiful flat stomach, and wondered again why girls defiled their bodies in such a way. In his view, tattoos made unattractive women ugly and beautiful women unattractive. Berenice did not have one and, again, he wondered if he should not be here and leave. Yet animal lust and the possibility of seizing a moment never proffered by Berenice was not easily resisted, and when she turned to him and put her hand on his very firm manhood, he knew he could not refuse, especially when she just lay on her back, her legs open and her juices apparent, softly pleading, "Please… go on…" And so he did…

Berenice arrived back at her flat and realised, in the upset of annoying Shuo and then trying to see and placate him, that she had forgotten to do a budget for the next day's early morning meeting, which made her even angrier: Shuo had upset not only her emotions but her schedule, too. She decided she was better off without him after all.

Chapter Three

—⁊⁊⁊—

The next morning at work, Berenice and Shuo managed to avoid each other without too much difficulty: she was in meetings and he managed to catch up with some unfinished jobs which needed resolving away from the building. At lunchtime, she went out to a shopping mall and bought some tasteless junk food, which was unlike her; yet she wanted to stay away from him for as long as possible to show her disdain. Actually, she did not know whether it was disdain or anger, she just suddenly grasped that her lack of experience with men of her own age was a disadvantage. Perhaps she was cut out for relationships with older men, she pondered, for her ability and intelligence were well beyond her years, and if she followed that course then it might mean more intellectual conversations and probably more attention, too; also, the ability to spend more time and money on the good things in life, as they would inevitably be richer. Shuo, as she so frequently told herself, was just a boy. Then, with a bump, she had to succumb to the fact that older men liked sex as much as young ones did – even more, if anything, as their opportunities were fewer. Her uncle had at least taught her that. She descended into her uneasy gloom again and sucked on her milkshake through a straw. It was quite disgusting.

Shuo was experiencing the same gamut of emotions, if from a different perspective. He could not ascertain whether his meeting with Lin Yang had been a wonderful one-off, the beginning of something amazing or a terrible mistake. He had enjoyed it, for sure – months of pent-up frustration whilst with Berenice had exploded into a passion of the most extraordinary sex he had ever encountered. She was voracious. And whilst he had managed to keep up with her due to his predicament, he wondered whether he would be able to sustain it long-term. At first, he had wondered if she was just out for some sex and that was all, but she also showed a tenderness and appreciation which surprised him; she genuinely seemed to like him, too, and kept on kissing him when he knew he had to go back to his flat at four in the morning, if only to shower, get into some fresh clothes and leave almost immediately for the office! They seemed to have a rapport: and when she said she regretted having had a tattoo, he warmed to her even more, for it showed she could learn from mistakes and had the capacity to assess things. He liked that. And although Berenice was capable of detailed polemic about almost any business or design subject, she kept most of it to herself, whereas Lin knew far less but was able to discuss what little she knew in a far more detailed way. Yet he found himself wishing that the events had been with Berenice and that her particular impasse had been broken; but then he felt grateful that providence had intervened and he had been gifted this beautiful young woman as a sort of consolation prize, however patronising he knew that sounded. He truly hoped it would last – especially long enough to prove that he would not ultimately miss Berenice – but of that he could not be sure.

His mind went back to the sex – he just could not stop thinking about it: it had been extraordinary. She could do things with her body and her mouth that he had never known about, and certainly never experienced before. Her breasts were broad-based but not too protuberant, her nipples dark and inviting with a juicy sweetness he had not tasted previously; her skin was smooth with a brownish tinge and her legs were perfect – better than Berenice's, in fact. She had beautifully formed extremities, too, which were varnished in a wild pink, only let down by the fact that the colour was chipped. Her hands were firm but tender when she rubbed his member, the colours blurring as her hands went up and down it with such a speed and delicate touch as to delight him into an uncontrollable ecstasy. She had teased him like this for several minutes, eventually turning onto her back and saying in a forthright but pleading way, "Please make love with me again!" And so they did.

Back in the office after lunch, the inevitable happened and he bumped into Berenice. They found themselves as awkward friends, each sparring to say something friendly yet trying to avoid the chance of saying anything that might betray what was on both their minds. They seemed to circle one another as they tried to both connect and also escape, and any observer would have noticed that they were both very pink in the face.

Being the more outspoken of the two, it was Berenice who eventually came to the point. "I went to your flat yesterday, after you left," she said, "but you weren't there." Shuo was astonished and did not instantly know how to respond. Seeing his confusion, and trying to trap him into a revealing answer, she added, "And I know you were there."

"Actually, I wasn't," Shuo stammered, attempting to get out of the way of the overweight CEO who was passing with his assistant at that moment. He noticed that Berenice gave him an exaggerated smile as he passed, which annoyed him, but once they were gone she turned back to him as he said, "Look, I think we'd better go somewhere private. I don't want—"

"So where were you, then?" she enquired more harshly. "I tried to ring you quite late. Are you avoiding me?"

Shuo put a hand on her shoulder and guided her into a recess where the watercooler stood, a little further down the corridor. "I stayed with a friend," he replied shiftily, unable to look her straight in the eye. There was a pause as his gaze returned uncertainly to hers, and away again.

She was fairly certain she knew what that meant: but she would play the dumb woman for a little longer as her beautiful big brown eyes bored into his mind. "I missed you," she said simply, with a subtle but steely resolve. Actually, as she said it, she wondered if she actually meant it, but it did not matter as she wanted to make him feel awkward. Which she was.

Then, unexpectedly, and with the unlikely advantage of suddenly finding there was momentarily nobody anywhere near them, he found his confidence and looked straight at her, saying, "Look, Berenice, you know I wanted to love you but you wouldn't let me; we've been seeing each other for months yet we've never... never, you know..."

"Had sex?"

Her forthrightness surprised him. "Well, yes," he replied.

"Is that more important than my mind, the fact we get on well, that we enjoy the same things and are easy in each other's company?" she interrogated, with a hint of mockery suffused with teasing.

"No; but having gone so far, and getting on so well, like you say, it's time we became a 'proper' couple," he said awkwardly. Then added: "You're always putting it off. I can't wait forever."

"I see. Well, let's talk about it later. Not here. Tonight. I'll come round to you after work. Make sure your flat's tidy, for once. I'll see you at seven." And with that, she turned away and went back to her work. Shuo was stunned. She had regained control, just when he thought he had made a point and become the dominant party for the first time. Yet he couldn't see her tonight – he was seeing Lin Yang.

Berenice went back to her desk and immersed herself in her work, yet found it difficult: she was distracted and wondered if she had made a mess of her life. She was pretty sure of what had happened, whether he had been in his flat or not; what she did not know was whether this had been going on at the same time as he was seeing her, which would have angered her. No, it *did* anger her, because she *didn't* know. She had lost control: Shuo had found another girl, who had given him sex. She should have seen it coming, she chided herself. A good-looking young boy with a pleasant character and fun demeanour would always be attractive to women. Then, with a shiver of horror, she wondered if the girl worked in the same building: perhaps she knew Berenice and was trying to compromise her? What if she was senior in position to her, so would be even more attractive to Shuo? Well, that would make her work harder to keep him – as long as it did not compromise her work, of course, the most important aspect of her life. Yet she could not tell Shuo of her early sexual experiences because, even now, it was all too raw. The thought of something inside her again was a painful prospect, both physically and mentally, and would bring back so many terrifying fears and memories that she wondered if she could ever cope. Yet she would have to confront it some day. Perhaps even tonight? No, she would hold him off a little longer. And he was not really good enough for her, she had to admit once more: so was he worth it anyway? Well, she would see him and make up her mind. After all, she had to find out more about this girl: and she was sure her own intellect and beauty could outshine anyone's. That's what everyone said, and she relished believing it.

Meanwhile, Shuo was in a state of panic and himself discombobulated. He did not want to stop Berenice coming round, especially if tonight would, at last, be 'the night', but he did not know how he could put off Lin Yang. Nor, after last night, did he know whether he wanted to. Berenice was so controlling, so positive, so always right about everything – but classier than Lin Yang. Yet Yang had a mystique that he could not explain: perhaps because he only knew her physically rather than mentally at this moment, whereas with Berenice it was the other way round. It might have been easier if one had been prettier than the other, but they were both beautiful – if in different ways – and in his realisation of that he wondered if he should just introduce them to each other and let them fight it out over him. No – Berenice would win; she was far more intelligent. But then, he had no idea what sex would be like with Berenice. Perhaps he never would. He would give her one last chance – it was tonight or that was it. After that, he would make his decision. He picked up the phone and rang Lin Yang's mobile to ask if they could postpone until tomorrow. Infuriatingly, it went to voicemail. He was annoyed – he had tried to make a decision but was unable to follow it through.

In a different part of the same building, Berenice was trying to suppress a variety of conflicting emotions and the thought kept taunting her that two people in close proximity were experiencing similar emotional feelings but from a different standpoint: one out of fear, the other out of possible disappointment. Unlike Shuo, she could clearly see both sides of the situation…

What neither of them knew was that, in the late afternoon sunshine, Lin Yang was waiting for Shuo outside the building already. She had done herself up, too, and looked stunningly beautiful: she did not want to lose him.

Chapter Four

—✺—

Berenice closed her laptop and looked at the clock: it was time to leave in a couple of minutes, so she would go to the rest-rooms and ensure she looked her best, which would fill the time nicely. How dare Shuo think he could terminate their relationship just like that!

At the same time, Shuo entered the foyer, ostensibly to ensure that Berenice would not change her mind and do a runner – but the first person he saw as he arrived was Lin Yang. He was both elated and horrified: Berenice was punctual to the second and would arrive at any moment, yet here, unexpectedly, was Lin Yang – looking exquisite, demure and utterly beautiful, with a presence that had been unexpected in the whirlwind of yesterday. Finding an inner strength he had never had before, he swept up to her, put his arm around her and – before they had even had a chance to say anything – escorted her outside. She tried to kiss him but he resisted, saying he could not be seen kissing a girl outside his firm's offices as it would be used against him. For a moment, she stopped, then decided to allow Shuo to whisk her to the privacy of the building's side: but it was just too late to prevent Berenice seeing them disappear through the revolving doors. She had only seen a glimpse of a stockinged female leg, but Shuo was unmistakable and she knew immediately what had happened.

Outside, Shuo was desperately trying to tell Lin Yang – despite his resistance to do so – that he had to postpone. "I tried to ring you to say I can't make it tonight after all," he said awkwardly.

"I had the day off," she replied, a smile playing across her cherry-red lips. "Last night exhausted me."

Shuo was pleasantly shocked – Berenice would never have admitted that even if it had actually happened. "Look," he continued, "I have to see someone regarding work, so why don't you go somewhere – a bar, or—"

"I'm not going to a bar on my own," she protested. "And anyway, how long will you be?"

"Only an hour or two. Please – it's for my future; it's important. Go home and I'll join you later."

"Promise?"

"Promise."

She pecked him on the cheek, moved away, looked back at him and then said coyly, "See you later, then," and disappeared into the homebound throng of people. Shuo sighed and looked after her for a moment, then turned round. On the steps outside the doors was Berenice, and she had seen everything.

—⁊⁊⁊—

Lin Yang, slightly discomfited, decided to look at some shops for an hour and then go home to await Shuo. She would cook him a nice meal, she thought, then the rest of the evening would take care of itself. She bought some pork, some dumplings and a bottle of wine, a new pair of shoes, and a couple of candles. Then she saw a nice tablecloth and thought that it would enhance her little dinner table for that evening and bought it. She went into a bar, bought herself a drink to quell the butterflies running riot in her stomach, and enjoyed putting down a young nerd who tried his luck with her. Then she loftily left and slowly made her way home to prepare for what was going to be a wonderful evening. For the first time in her life she felt confident and optimistic: meeting Shuo had turned her from a silly girl into a paragon of common sense and young womanhood, and she had never felt so good in her life.

—m—

"Who was that?" was the tart response from Berenice as Shuo approached her. Shuo, not at first realising that she had seen the whole tiny episode – the placating, the coy smiles, the peck on the cheek, the obvious intimacy – was confounded for a moment but suddenly the situation again gave him a strength and sense of purpose he had hitherto lacked: he calmly just put his hand on her shoulder, kissed her lightly on her beautiful nose and said, "Just a friend." Berenice was stumped: he had never been so composed in what she saw as a moment of adversity. He just stared at her with a look on his face that said, 'What's the fuss about?', took her arm and led her in the opposite direction to the one Lin Yang had taken. Never having been in this situation with Shuo before, where he was definitely in charge, Berenice found herself unsure what to say or do next as she meekly followed him towards a shopping centre where he knew there was an ice-cream parlour she liked.

Once they had sat down and he had bought her favourite delight without even asking if she wanted it, her question 'How long have you known her?' seemed to hover in the air without any sense of expecting an answer – whether it was even a lie or the truth; so when Shuo, looking around rather than straight at her as he usually did, didn't answer, she decided not to push it and just believe him. For now, at least. What was gnawing at her stomach was that she had never seen him like this before and – worse – she suddenly realised she found his new confidence and firm offhandedness rather compelling. And, she was shocked to admit to herself, sexy.

For his part, Shuo was in torment; his apparent *sangfroid* was actually a terror of saying or giving away anything. He did not know what to do or how to react, so he just found himself feigning being distant, unphased and, in common parlance, 'cool'. Yet because Berenice did not know how to react either, she suddenly felt a release, as if she could suddenly let Shuo do anything with her and she would not mind – even, she shuddered as she admitted to herself – to go back and allow him to instantly make passionate love to her. In an instant, she suddenly realised she loved him; why had she been so stupid to withhold him all this time? Or was this just a convoluted way of her innermost soul trying to take back control by perversely allowing him to do just what he wanted? Her permission, her acceptance, her submission?

Shuo, meanwhile, was desperately assessing his options beneath a veneer of facial indifference. He could not let Lin Yang down; in less than twenty-four hours he had met – and instinctively got to know, almost without trying – another girl whose very being attuned with his. He had gone further with her and got to know her faster yet more deeply in one evening than several months with Berenice… but was that a good or a bad thing? He didn't know. Yet Berenice was the class of girl he aspired to: he wanted to be with someone whom he could look up to. Lin Yang had uncovered herself – in every way – on their first meeting. How much more was there to know about her? *Was* there anything more to know about her? Would it last? He turned to Berenice, who was uncharacteristically looking vacantly out in front of her, a spoonful of ice-cream hovering uncertainly before her lips as if she was unsure whether to allow its continuation to its destination.

Shuo spoke: "Berenice, I wasn't expecting to see you again… well, outside work, I mean. You were so offhand yesterday afternoon… you just don't seem to appreciate me. I just thought that you didn't want to see me any more…" She looked up at him, put the spoon in her mouth and took the ice-cream, then made to speak – but Shuo continued before she could do so: "I think we need some time apart. Even if it's only a few days… Just to see how we feel – how things pan out. It's not a decision I've taken lightly, but…"

A decision! Shuo had made a decision, which affected Berenice! The cheek! *She* made the decisions and he did what he was told! That was how she had always planned it: *her* decision – there was no going back on that. She was more literate, articulate and sensible than he was; how could he run their lives if they got married? Married! That was a word that she had never even contemplated before, and here it was presenting itself in her brain – what was going on? He had just said they should spend some time apart and suddenly she was thinking of life's arch-commitment!

In her flurry of unexpected emotions, she then realised that Shuo was talking to her – in a detached, disparate way. She focussed on his face, and his lips were saying, "...so I need to go home tonight and think about things – you, me – and that'll give us the time to assess things and come to the right conclusion. I do love you, Berenice; but you have to prove that you love me, too."

Berenice just nodded, shell-shocked and trembling at this new, unwelcome experience. Then she felt Shuo kissing her lightly on her lips and his presence evaporated. She sat there for a good twenty seconds before she finally realised he had gone, leaving this beautiful, newly vulnerable girl sitting in the middle of a busy ice-cream parlour on a tall stool, like a threatened lighthouse in the midst of a turbulent sea.

Outside, Shuo stopped for a moment and nearly went back, but thought better of it as he recognised what had previously eluded him: that he had just found the key to power over the woman he loved. Yet as he contemplated that, he found himself imagining the certain delights of the carnal night he had ahead of him, and his step quickened away from the embattled Berenice.

Chapter Five

—◊—

The next morning, Berenice did not turn up for work. She had lain awake most of the night, trying to balance what she felt about Shuo's explanation. She had realised that it would take her a long time to find someone as loyal as him, and had wrestled with the premise that she might never find someone to get on with as easily she did him. Yes, it was all very well being intelligent, attractive and beautiful but – as she had found in the past – that was a double-edged sword. She could attract men with ease but were they the right type? And what if her innate resistance to men – based on her own feeling of superiority, if not ability to connect sexually – came to the fore again? Would she then miss Shuo as the best man she had never had, in all senses of the word?

Her dilemma still unresolved by the small hours, she decided she could not see Shuo and, having several days of untaken holiday, decided to use some of them on the pretence that an aunt had suddenly been taken ill the night before and she had to catch a very early flight to Chengdu to see her. So she rang the office at five and left a message on her boss's number to tell him – there would be no-one there at that hour – then went back to bed with a cup of tea. Sitting there with nothing to do except think of her situation was something she had never experienced before and however hard she urged herself to 'forget Shuo and go back to sleep' her will to do so was at odds with her ability to ignore it. Was this love? Or resentment? Anger, perhaps? Displaced seniority? She turned over and eventually went to sleep an hour or two afterwards.

However, four hours later she was woken by her telephone ringing in the hallway. But she could not answer it – she was supposedly on a flight to Chengdu! Then she wondered if it was Shuo; no, it was almost ten o'clock and the office would have told him she was going off to see her aunt in Chengdu. So could it be Shuo? It would not be her boss – but when just about to risk picking up, she also remembered she had lied: she didn't have an aunt in Chengdu. She had said it to service her deceit and Shuo might have unwittingly mentioned that fact. And she was not in the mood to substantiate her dishonesty to him under the circumstances as it would prove to him that she was upset and had lied to cover it up. Anyway, she just wanted to be left alone… So she let it ring and, when it stopped, the echo seemed to decay slowly down the hallway as if resonating her own despair. Yes, that was what it was – despair. She was missing something – but once again wondering whether it was due to Shuo or her sense of pique, she really could not tell…

—w—

Contrary to Berenice, Lin Yang felt on top of the world. She had barely noticed her trip into work on the Beijing subway, which, with its noisy adverts on the ubiquitous screens, was normally a time of extended torment for her. When she arrived at work, two people said how well and lovely she looked, and her smile radiated in all directions. Her job as a graphic designer and artist for an online news channel was one she loved, and although the main news was depressing that day – a plane crash outside Beijing on its way to Chengdu where all the passengers, bar one, had been killed, along with the entire crew – did not dent her feeling of elation. She was sure she was in the first flush of love, which was a novel sensation for her; but she was careful not to let it carry her away. It was early days yet and she was intelligent enough to know that much could happen to spoil it all but, at this moment, she was ecstatically happy and nothing was going to get her down. More pictures and video footage of the crash started to come in during the morning, but although many of the images were horrific she could not stop thinking about Shuo, whose smiling face seemed always to be between her and the screen. Her second night with him had been as wonderful as expected, despite her finding him somewhat quieter and more withdrawn than he had been the previous time; perhaps he had been as worried as she had by the overwhelming intensity of their relationship, but as soon as the dinner she cooked had been eaten and they were in bed together it was like being in an enchanted garden full of exotic and unknown flowers and experiences. For both of them.

For his part, Shuo was torn and did not know what to do. His journey to work had been uncomfortable and he found himself looking around furtively in the office in case Berenice suddenly appeared. He wanted to speak to her but didn't dare, and hoped he would not bump into her. For although his night with Lin Yang had been incredible again, he had not been able to get Berenice out of his mind: indeed, the whole time he was making love with Yang, Berenice's prim and disapproving face had been omnipresent. Yet the experience with Yang was so wonderful that he could not have stopped it even if he had wanted to: again, it had been extraordinary. She had instinctively pushed the boundaries of love-making even further – adopting positions and creating sensations which even exceeded those she had performed the night before. And yet... he wondered whether, if he had ever managed to find himself in the same situation with Berenice, would it have been as astonishing as what he was now getting used to? Or better? The statistics on his computer in front of him were swimming before his eyes, every movement seeming to reveal another facet of Yang's beautiful body and what she could do with it: it was as if she was there in front of him, teasing him with as-yet-untried pleasures as he remembered those that he had just encountered.

It was now approaching one o'clock so he decided to get a snack – he was ravenously hungry for some reason – and went down in a different lift to the one Berenice would have used. He bought a rice-cake and ate it as if an automaton, chewing distractedly as humanity swirled around him. At one point, a friend came over and broke into his thoughts, asking how Berenice was as he had not seen her at work that morning. This question cut through: she had not been seen at work that morning? This man sat almost opposite her –

surely she would have told this man if she was taking time off or going away? Or Shuo? No, she probably would not have told him, after last night… The man was still prattling in front of him, but he, and what he was saying, were a blur. Shuo felt a little sick: had she done something silly – like give up her job because of him…? Or perhaps something worse? Was she all right, he wondered? And if not, was it his fault? A wave of remorse washed over him and he was aware he had tears in his eyes. He realised he was still in love with her and looked up to address the man opposite – but he had given up trying to gain Shuo's attention and had disappeared. He decided to go past her office on the way back to his own – just to prove to himself that she was not there and it was not a ploy from Berenice to get him to come and see her. She did things like that; it was her way of keeping him under control.

So he went to Berenice's part of the building and nonchalantly walked through its corridors and, as he passed her office, cast an eye at where she usually sat: no, she wasn't there. The man who had been trying to engage with him in the snack bar saw him observing Berenice's empty space but turned away as Shuo looked at him.

Returning to his desk, Shuo saw Mr. Chen, his boss, waiting for him, who had an unusually concerned look on his face. Shuo was just about to apologise for not being at his post when the man held up his hand and just said quietly, "Shuo, come into my office, will you? I have something to discuss with you," and left.

Shuo followed behind and when they arrived at his office he wondered why Mr. Chen had not asked his assistant, Natalya, to fetch him; it was all very odd.

"Close the door," he instructed him, and as the buzz of the office hushed when he did so, he suddenly felt very vulnerable. Was he about to be sacked?

"You and Berenice are close, I believe," he stated, partly as a question and partly for confirmation.

"Er, yes," Shuo replied, not having realised that his boss knew about their relationship.

"Have you spoken to her today?" Mr. Chen continued.

When Shuo shook his head, he suddenly found himself panicking – was a relationship with a person technically senior to himself not allowed? Or had Berenice decided to destroy his reputation in pique for having cooled their affair and he was being dismissed?

"Well, you must have known she was flying to Chengdu today, I suppose?"

"Chengdu? No."

"Ah. Well she left a message on my voicemail here very early this morning to say her aunt in Chengdu had been taken ill and she was flying up to see her – she sounded quite upset so I think it might be serious."

"I didn't know she had an aunt in Chengdu," Shuo retorted, then mentally kicked himself for saying it as he would never have wanted to betray Berenice, whatever she was about to do to him.

"Hm. Well, I don't want to presuppose anything or worry you, but you've probably also heard that there's been an air crash this morning – and it was a flight to Chengdu."

Shuo suddenly felt weak and dizzy, and asked if he could sit down.

Mr. Chen went out and brought back some water in a flimsy paper cup, then continued. "I'm sorry but, er, and I don't want to make this worse for you, but there was only one survivor – and obviously no-one knows yet who that was. But…"

Shuo felt terrible; the office was spinning around him and he felt as if he hadn't eaten for weeks, he felt so faint.

"Of course, there are a number of flights to the city but there's only one in the early morning and therefore we must suppose that it could have been the one Berenice was on."

There was a long pause, and Shuo found himself gasping, tears streaming down his face, as he struggled to make sense of the situation. "Thank you for telling me, sir," he mumbled.

Mr. Chen was already telling him he would organise a car to take him home so he could be alone, and that he could take tomorrow off at least to have a chance to find out about her and sort things out. "Just keep me informed and if you hear any news, please let me know immediately," he said finally, followed by, "I'm very sorry to have had to tell you this. There is still a glimmer of hope, but…"

Shuo found himself nodding and murmuring thank-yous and kindnesses to his boss for being so understanding as he struggled to his feet, went slowly back to his desk and, collecting his bag, went out the front to await the car his boss had promised. Well, that was probably it, he thought; at least he would not have to now go through the torment of making a choice; he had Lin Yang now and he would make the most of it, whatever. Then he chided himself for being so callous and was in floods of tears as the car whisked him away.

Chapter Six

—⚊—

Berenice had eventually left her bed and stomped around her flat for a while before deciding to go out and cheer herself up with some shopping. She would have seen friends but did not really have any; she was everybody's friend, she always said to herself, so why tie yourself down to one or two? Shuo was her friend, and the rest of her social life was taken up by work matters. That was how she liked it. Then she had a jolt as she remembered Shuo had decided not to be her friend any more. Possibly. Probably, even. With that, she found herself having a little weep – whether for her scorned pride or for missing him, she still wasn't sure – then dried her eyes and told herself to show some inner strength and rise above these sentimental emotions. Work and advancement were more rewarding; she would prevail, she assured herself… and then burst into tears again.

A couple of hours later, she was sitting in one of the newly fashionable restaurants which were slowly replacing the more traditional establishments that were solely there for eating, with their cold, garish, fluorescent lights, mops and luridly-coloured buckets in the corner, wires everywhere, and negligible service at odds with the food they served. No, this was one of Beijing's more affluent establishments, with linen tablecloths, good cutlery and crockery, smart waiters and a definite ambiance; she liked it. The bustle of the newly-rich young things buzzed around her and she started to feel better. After two exceptionally good glasses of French wine (it said so on the menu and were also very expensive), she felt better still. But she was alone. That word, 'alone' resonated around her head, even as the hubbub seemed to counteract it, embracing her like a soft duvet, giving warmth and comfort. She found herself observing the people around her, something her egocentric soul had seldom done before, and she realised there was a bigger social world out there than she had previously ever bothered to contemplate. There were even some nice-looking young men, all busily talking to girlfriends; business associates and overweight bosses, too, with their wives and attendant concupiscent younger women – mistresses; she disdained them. Yet she was more beautiful than all of them – but despite this, just not part of anyone's life now. Single, unloved and friendless. She had tried calling her mother in Chengdu without any intention of telling her why other than to pass some time but her mother, as usual, was out and Berenice chided herself for thinking she would have been either sympathetic or warm to her and would anyway have preferred to go and play mah-jong with her friends – which was probably what she was doing. Compulsory state retirement at sixty in China had produced swathes of older women who did little more than eat out in huge groups in restaurants or play China's national game in large groups at each others' homes. Berenice would never allow herself to become like that, she resolved, and that was that.

Across the restaurant, she suddenly noticed a man sitting alone who seemed to be subtly observing her; he was obviously Western, with kind eyes and a sweet smile, which she observed when he spoke to the waitress – probably American or, even, English, as he seemed to have reserve and an apparent intellectual demeanour not usually associated with the former. She found herself stealing looks at him; probably quite a bit older than herself, she thought, perhaps fifteen years or even more. But he seemed young for his age, despite his smart dress, which was pleasant without being ostentatious.

Her waitress arrived and she decided to have a sweet, guiltily realising that she was only doing so to prolong her stay. The waitress disappeared and she stole another look towards this man who had encroached on her consciousness. But her heart sank when she saw that he had gone.

—∞—

Shuo was in a state of deepest worry. He had tried phoning Berenice to see if she was all right, but after leaving several messages he concluded that her phone had been switched off, she had blocked his calls… or she and the phone were dead at the bottom of a pile of aircraft wreckage. Then his phone rang and his heart soared – but it was Lin Yang. He found himself to be strangely detached from her but could not explain to her the reasons why – his emotions were in turmoil; he was still not even sure himself what he felt. As he had the day off – again he did not tell Lin Yang why – she said she would leave work early and they arranged to meet in an hour or two: but he finished the call with more brevity than she had been used to. This made her wonder if she had done something wrong yet could not think of anything, which made her quiet and introverted. Then, with a rush of decisive determination, she stood up, took a deep breath and indignantly decided to push the boat out when she saw him: she would go home and make herself look even more stunning than she had ever attempted before. She wasn't going to lose Shuo that soon or so easily.

Chapter Seven

—꧁—

Berenice, slightly unstable on her high heels after a larger consumption of wine than she was used to, left the restaurant and emerged blinking into the bright sunlight of an uncharacteristically clear Beijing day. There was blossom on the trees and a breeze blew her skirt and blouse against her body, momentarily outlining her figure. She was pleased no-one was around to notice: even if she knew she had a good body, she was decorous enough not to wish to show it off to anyone. Even when she had been with Shuo, she liked to dress discreetly so as not to flaunt herself. That came by other means – the coy look, the glanced smile with the wry promise of more, the look away then back, and all the other armoury she instinctively had as a young woman. But Shuo was no more; she would have to start all over again and find someone as malleable, forgiving and… well, understanding as he had been. Or stupid. She chastised herself for that last thought: he wasn't stupid, just naïve sometimes, but she had managed to exploit that in her own manipulative way. She stepped off the pavement to cross the road and, blinded for a second by the bright sunlight, did not see a dark, sleek limousine coming towards her. The screech of brakes made her jump back and – already being unstable on her feet – she turned her ankle on one of her high heels and fell between two cars, grazing her elbow and tearing her tights on her right leg. Within a second, a man was standing over her offering a hand up, and a deep, mellifluous voice in gentlemanly English was asking if she was hurt.

In an instant, she realised it was the man whom she had observed in the restaurant.

—✺—

Shuo rang Lin Yang's doorbell at the base of her tower block and waited for a response. He had not heard any further news about the Chengdu plane crash and had decided it was all over and that he would never see Berenice again. Perhaps it was a lucky escape, he thought – she would have tormented him for years and he might never even have made love with her anyway. Not like Lin Yang, whose metallicised voice was now inviting him up as the buzzer rasped its welcome and the door clicked open.

He arrived at her apartment on the 23rd floor, knocked with his knuckles on the dusty paintwork and waited. Nothing. He knocked again. Still nothing. Usually, he would hear her heels clicking towards him across the wooden floor. What was she doing? Heightening the anticipation of seeing him, or trying to make him realise *he* should be lucky to see *her*? Then the door opened. Shuo had not taken so much care about his attire as normal and, in a split second, regretted it as a wave of perfume assailed his nostrils and he saw her, barefoot and in a beautiful traditional Chinese silk dress, standing before him. She just stood there, hoping and waiting her appearance would be such that he would just melt into her arms. In an instant, all thoughts of Berenice evaporated and he did just that.

Within seconds, her clothing was off and they were making noisy, passionate love on her bed; in the miasma of pleasure which followed, it was safe to say that Shuo thought little, if at all, of his previous concerns about Berenice. This, with Lin Yang, was serious and all that was over; in truth, he was so intoxicated by Lin Yang's sexuality that Berenice did not really stray into his consciousness at all. Beyond all expectation, Lin Yang had achieved her objective

—∿—

At much the same time, Berenice had arrived back at her flat and was now changing her ripped tights and scuffed heels, having first washed the gash on her arm sustained when she fell. She was moving purposefully, wanting to be quick; she re-applied her make-up and wondered what she was doing as she did so. After her fall, the man who had nearly killed her had ensured she was unhurt, helping her up and steadying her with a kindly but non-threatening arm around her waist. His voice was rich, soft, concerned; and he had the smell of fresh hay about him which she had not encountered since her time in the countryside where she had once gone to see her father. His voice was similar to her father's, too, and its resonance reached deep into her soul, comforting her. He had an aura which oozed gentle confidence and tallied with his nice looks, the eyes softly wrinkled due to laughter rather than worry and which somehow matched in colour the tone of his slightly sandy, thick hair which was parted on his left side, ensuring a firm hairline at the front. His hands were well-manicured and his shoes were clean – her mother would have liked that. This man had been, as she surmised when observing him, English; he was a businessman who spent a lot of time in China adapting Chinese or Western television shows for production in the other's country. He had had a big hit with a Western game show which he had successfully piloted in Beijing and which had become very successful – it must have been, as even Berenice had heard of it. Yet he had not appeared to be the sort of brash person she would have expected in this field, being cultured, considerate and literate.

He had introduced himself as George and offered her a lift home, which she had declined, as she did not know him – but had stayed in conversation with him as she recovered and regained her composure. In fact, it was difficult to stop talking to him: he not only had that lovely voice but was fascinating, attentive, courteous, witty, amusing and well-dressed. He loved classical music, English literature and, above all, the English countryside, which he was passionate about protecting. Berenice had never been to England but had seen pictures of its rural areas and been overcome by the beauty of its patchwork fields and subtle shapes and colours. She had also instinctively appreciated the sense of continuing tradition – something which had been increasingly expunged from China in its relentless quest for modernisation. Thanks to her father, Berenice loved English literature, too, especially poetry, and had read many classic novels and plays as well as more contemporary works by American and European writers, many of whom she found they both knew of. In short, she had realised that, despite the obvious age difference, she had an instinctive affinity with him.

Some of these details had come out as she recovered from her fright, wedged between the two cars; but the more personal ones emerged as he had driven her home. She had relented and he was now waiting for her outside.

Chapter Eight

—◊◊◊—

Shuo lay awake as Lin Yang slept beside him. In the half light, his eyes caressed her beautiful form, only spoilt, in his opinion, by the tattoo, which looked like a self-imposed birthmark that in previous times people would either try to remove or cover up – not pay for. Berenice would never have had one: she'd have said that personality was more important than a distraction such as that and once you had showed it off to your friends, that was the end of the conversation. And then you were stuck with the thing for the rest of your life. Then Berenice was overwhelming his thoughts again and he missed her – especially as he had concluded that he would never see her again. How could he? She was obviously dead. He had thought of making enquiries as to whom the sole survivor of the air crash was but knew that he would be in a long queue of worried people who had more claim to information than he had. A tear welled in his eye and dripped slowly down his cheek, leaving a tiny warm trail of sorrow as it reached his mouth, the salty taste adding a sense of piquancy to the moment.

The muffled sounds of the day were prominent outside as it was still only the middle of the evening: their passion had lasted for almost two hours and they had exhausted themselves. He wondered whether to get himself a drink and some sustenance to last him through the night, but then Lin Yang stirred, they started kissing, and soon the Elysium of bliss enveloped his thoughts, soul and conscience once more. She did not just lie there and be subservient – she initiated things. Unlike Berenice. There he was, he admonished himself – thinking of her again… Yang, noticing a momentary lull in his interest for her, dived under the covers and he was soon aware of his member being stroked and sucked in such a way that it was pleasurable to the point of pain, making it impossible to think of anything – and, especially in the mounting height of ecstasy – anyone else. Lin Yang's pertly pointed breasts alone were enough to make even the least aware man aroused, a thin circle of fainter-coloured skin encircling her smooth brown nipples which were perfected by a microscopic crater in the tip of each; then he was inside her again from behind, his thighs pounding into the heavenly space between her small, firm buttocks as the dark skin around her clitoris swept in and out with the movement. She was extraordinary… yet, in the intense excitement, he still wished he could have had – at least just once – the same experience with Berenice. For comparison, if not only for the sake of the conquest of the girl he had truly loved. How long would it be, he wondered, before he could get her out of his mind? Never, he concluded…

—ⵥ—

Outside Chengdu, the final dead body was being dragged from the wreckage, a beautiful young girl who was charred almost beyond recognition so it was impossible to match her face with the check-in video or passenger manifest. But if anyone had been there who had known Berenice, it could very well have been her… The only survivor was announced as a middle-aged lady from Beijing who had somehow been shielded from both the impact and the resulting flames by other people's bodies and was shocked but only lightly scarred. Miracles happen sometimes… but this one would not have been of any interest to Shuo.

Berenice was, in fact, sitting in front of George in a bar which looked out over the city; he liked this place in particular as it doubled as a library for Western books, if not always the greatest literature. It was also a place where usually beautiful, intellectually-inclined and well-dressed Chinese girls went to meet Western men, a sort of literary Ellis Island. It was perched at the top of an office building near the Workers' Stadium and reached by a four-part external metal staircase which became slippery in the wet: in addition, its large mesh made trips up and down somewhat tricky for the high heels which frequented its surface – particularly on the way down after a few drinks. The interior of the bar was cosy, intimate and lined with racks of books, some new and many second-hand – the latter observation which also described a number of expatriate men who frequented the place. In fact, George was probably one of them.

Yet Berenice did not mind: she was captivated by him. He was a fund of stories, jokes and information, especially about writers and the literature they wrote. She was a fan of

Oscar Wilde and was delighted when George announced that he was too, subsequently regaling her with anecdotes about the author she had never heard. It did not bother her that she knew she might see him again and – for once – was happily hoping for it; she did not dare to ask if he was married for fear that this would put an end to the evening by implication if he was. For the first time in her life, indeed, she felt she was not in control of her life but did nothing to resist it: and it sent a thrill through her body as she realised it.

As the evening progressed she became increasingly entranced – they just got on and it was all so delightfully easy: no embarrassed pauses, no wondering what to say next. The conversation just flowed – as did the drinks. Half-way through the evening she had had a fleeting panic when she found for an instant that he was reminding her of her predatory uncle and she had a sudden impulse to go… but George seemed so benign, honourable and kind, exposing no malicious intent; and his homely rationality produced an aura which confounded any feelings of trepidation so completely that these concerns were soon engulfed by a wave of warmth which smothered them entirely.

And almost without realising any implications, she just knew she would sleep with him. Sometime, if not tonight. And the prospect sent a thrill of abandonment through her body which she had never experienced before.

Chapter Nine

—⁂—

Mr. Chen Rudong, Shuo's boss, looked at the annual performance figures with some concern; the Design and Promotion department which Berenice had worked in had not come up to scratch recently, and yet her specific figures had been excellent. He, like most people in the office, had appreciated Berenice as a superb worker who had helped create many wonderful items which had sold across the world, and she was respected as a cold but impressive employee whom all the women cowered in front of – and all the men wanted to take to bed. Yet rumour had it that Shuo was her lover, although few could understand why she had chosen him: he was a pleasant, nice-looking boy but nothing exceptional. As a result, a few had risked making a pass at Berenice – although those who had were always summarily resisted – with the result that this often caused awkwardness when they needed company discourse with her. The word was that she was calculating, brilliant, always beautifully-attired but frigid. In fact, some were sorry for Shuo, who was well-liked but thought of as a lightweight;

they nonetheless felt happier when they concluded she must be using him and would cast him aside when she got a better offer – perhaps from a rich foreigner. Yet when they heard that it seemed likely she had been killed in a plane crash, the sympathy for Shuo was intense; sadly, no-one knew where he was in order to be able to console him. Also, being on what is known in the West as compassionate leave was unusual in China: in most companies, one was there to work and any sentimentality – however close a deceased friend or relative was – was taboo. And it made many in Mr. Chen's department realise that their boss was a decent man who cherished emotions, which they respected him for.

Yet this compassionate man now had a problem: Berenice was obviously dead so he needed to replace her: but he had to accept the hard truth that there was no-one in the company he could trust and rely on as he had done with her. She had had that wonderful ability to choose the right materials, firms and creatives to make beautiful things and draw everyone together: to ensure they were made exquisitely, cheaply yet with quality. Clients loved her and she had that ability to make men – and women – feel that there was an underlying attraction; she was an implicit tease which he knew she had affected for that purpose – because he knew that in reality she was actually cold and calculating. But making the clients feel that good was gold dust. He sighed deeply: now she was gone.

—∿—

After his latest carnal night with Lin Yang, Shuo felt elated and on top of the world. Her sexual prowess, beauty and ability to communicate was engulfing him and, despite initial reservations after hearing the news about Berenice, he felt grateful that he had met her. She knew how to make the most of him and combat his insecurities, always making him laugh and guiding him away from any potential disagreements. No, she was not subservient like many more traditional Chinese girls would be: she just had an instinct which concurred with his. He decided to go back to work the next morning.

Yet being in the same building and offices again would be difficult... and he was instantly cognisant of the fact he would miss Berenice's pervasive intellect and all-encompassing presence, as well as her subtle but engulfing scent, if not her frigidity. There was nothing he could do, though; although her death had not been officially confirmed – the government was not allowing names to be released for some reason – it still seemed more than likely she was gone. In any sense of the word...

Chapter Ten

—〰—

It had been wonderful: her well of fears and insecurities had evaporated like a spring mist. George's gentle understanding had dispersed all the angst of her early years spent in fear of her uncle or any feelings of hostility to older men – which, she realised with a feeling of release, had been lurking under the surface of her personality almost since she had gained cognisance of what that awful man had been doing to her. Yet with George, he never forced anything upon her: when he found her hesitant he had waited, talked more of other things to take her mind off her doubts and then, usually, made her laugh – ah, the laughter! What a tonic that was after the intensity of her time with Shuo and the horrors of her uncle! So much had been discussed that first night that she wondered if they might run out of things to talk about, but even after one evening she knew that this would never be the case. He had introduced her to the world and she now knew she could conquer it with him. Yet there were two subjects which she had avoided: the first – her uncle – out of embarrassment and disgust; the second – because she had not wished to sully the ecstasy of the evening – whether he had a wife back in England or not. Or a mistress here in Beijing, even. Well, if he did, she would ensure that she, the new Berenice, would replace her!

And when it had come to asking her back to his beautiful flat in San Li Tun, the international district of the city, she felt a sense of arrival – and what she had been instinctively but unknowingly waiting for over many years. Here she was, at the age of twenty-eight, suddenly in harmony with her life and where she was going in the world. George was the key, and she was not going to lose him. They had left the bar late – but not too much so – and carefully descended the external staircase: at one point, a heel had caught in the mesh and she almost tipped forward out of her shoe, but George had been anticipating the event and firmly but gently grasped her round the waist – not by another part of her anatomy as a supposedly accidental way of exploring her, as many men would have done. Shuo had tried that once and it had generated an unpleasant feeling between them for a number of days. His was the impulsiveness of youth, she admitted, but George's worldliness was a foil to that and she felt emotionally serene being with a gentleman more attuned to her adulthood than a mere boy could be.

George had neither invited her back to his flat, nor had she expected it – the subject was not discussed. It was just as if they both knew that something had happened and did not need to. Having waited outside hers while she had readjusted her make-up and changed her tights, he knew exactly where she lived and, as it happened, his flat – not far from the bar – was on the way to her area anyway. So

Berenice instinctively knew that an invitation to see where he lived was being made when he had stopped the car outside his block.

He just looked at her and she looked back with a doe-eyed smile on her face: nothing was said and he just turned into the underground carpark, they went up in the lift and they entered his home. He invited her to sit down on the leather sofa while he fixed a non-alcoholic drink: how did he know that was what she wanted after an evening in a bar? For him, he did not want to be accused of getting her drunk for sex, which could come back to bite either of them: no, it was just understood. He returned with two clinking glasses of elderflower cordial, an English drink which was new to her. He sat by her side but slightly apart, as if respecting her distance, and they each took a sip, their free hands inadvertently touching on the sofa; a thrill went through each of their bodies as it had not been intentional on either part – it just seemed programmed to happen and did. The hands instinctively clasped together, they looked into each other's eyes and then their moist lips touched, their mouths opening, so giving way to exploring tongues gyrating in slow, circular motions.

But nothing was rushed: kissing slowly, passionately and with feeling, Berenice found herself transported away from all her prejudices and the past; she felt a free woman at last. Nothing was said – they each knew what the other meant without saying... and when the clothes started to come off she did not resist but allowed the indulgence to take its course. Soon, almost without realising, they were in the bedroom and both naked on the bed: "I want to," she breathed, as she found herself grasping his very hard member. Then, feeling its girth, she whispered: "How am I going to fit that inside me? It might hurt me too much."

"If it does, I'll stop," he murmured back. Then, with a tiny cry of pleasure from Berenice, he was inside her and gently pulsating in and out of her, stimulating her clitoris each time his penis moved forward in such a way that she moaned with uncontrollable pleasure. *So this is what sex is really like*, she thought. *It's true – it's wonderful!* And in one sense she wondered whether she should have tried it with Shuo. But after several climaxes he was as far away in her mind as he had ever been.

—m—

Shuo went into work and made a request to see his boss, to thank him for his compassion and to say that he would like to get back to the office, despite the emotions of being in the same environment Berenice had been. On his way in, he was surprised to see Mr. Chen's assistant, Natalya, actually at her desk – an unusual situation. She was the building's spy, gossip and tell-tale, and she disliked everyone – as everyone did her. She particularly loathed Shuo, it seemed, for no reason he could imagine, except that she knew he had been involved with Berenice. Perhaps she was jealous – but whether of him or Berenice he had no idea: and nor did he care. He passed her as quickly as possible.

"So, you haven't heard from her?" Mr. Chen enquired, with a hint of despair in his voice. Shuo shook his head. "I see there was only one survivor and I doubt very much that it was Berenice," he stated gravely. "I've tried to find out, but they're being very tight with the details..." He paused, as if contemplating the reason, then continued, "Quite apart from the fact that she was brilliant and lovely in every way – as I hardly need to tell you," he added as confirmation, "her death has also left me with a problem..." He continued, but Shuo could, from then on, only hear a confused mumbling as the significance of the word 'death' suddenly seemed so final, brutal and immutable, and his experiences with Berenice crowded in on him. His boss was still talking when Shuo resurfaced from his unenforced and painful reverie to hear the final part of his sentence, which was, "...so I'll have to replace her. And that will be difficult."

He stared at Shuo, who suddenly looked broken. "I'm sorry," he said. "I do tend to go on a bit."

"Replace her?" Shuo enquired uncertainly.

"Well, yes, of course. I'll have to. But it'll be incredibly difficult. Berenice was unique."

There was a pause as the truth of that statement set in. Then, without thinking, Shuo blurted out, "Have you anyone in mind?" A wild idea had come into his head. If no-one would ever see Berenice again, then...

Mr. Chen shrugged and shook his head.

"I think I might know someone," Shuo said airily.

"And who is that?"

Shuo hesitated, then: "It's a lady I met a few days ago; she seems very intelligent... she works as a graphics artist and designer so she can draw beautifully – and has great ideas with colour..."

Mr. Chen just looked at him but said nothing: Shuo seemed to know a fair amount about this person and was so effusive in his boyish way that he wondered if Shuo had been seeing her before Berenice's demise – and for some time longer than the 'few days' he mentioned…

With Chen's eyes quizzically staring at him, Shuo felt he was being interrogated without a word being spoken, so continued: "And she likes fashion."

"There are very few girls who don't like fashion," he interjected wryly. "What experience does she have? She'd have to be damn good to replace Berenice. I mean, I could get Fang to step in – at least she worked with Berenice in her office."

"I don't think Berenice allowed her to do much," Shuo replied. "She liked to keep things to herself."

Chen looked at him, trying to read between the lines.

"May I give her a call and explain the job to her?"

There was a pause, then Chen said unconvincingly, "You can try. But remember that I haven't had absolute confirmation of Berenice's death yet. I'm sure she must have died as – probably like you – no-one has been able to contact her since the plane crash. I'm waiting for official confirmation that she was actually on the plane's passenger list, but that could take ages. You know how long official channels take – and at first they tried to rebuff me, too, by asking why I needed to know. I even had to prove I was her employer. But they still wouldn't tell me. Madness." He sighed and looked for a moment into space, then sat up straight, put his elbows on the desk and, looking at Shuo intently, continued, "So don't over-promise anything to this girl because first, I have to know conclusively that Berenice is dead and, secondly, she'll almost certainly not be suitable. It took me ages to find Berenice, and she'll be a very hard act to follow."

Shuo knew he was probably right, but thought it was worth a try, even though he did not like his boss's tone – this man did not know Lin Yang well enough to make those assumptions… mind you, nor did he, actually. At least from a professional perspective. But perhaps Lin Yang *was* more intelligent and adaptable than he was aware: one never knew so early on in a relationship.

"I'll give her a call, sir."

"OK. What's her name?"

"Lin Yang."

"Let me know how the conversation goes, then get back to me."

Shuo agreed and hurriedly left. On the way down to his desk, Shuo pondered his conversation with Mr. Chen and wondered what he had done. Was it madness? This girl whom he hardly knew, except from a sexual and instinctive context, working with him in the same office? The hurricane that was Lin Yang meant that the exact details of what work she did had not really been discussed. But he thought that – with some help from Berenice's pretty but fey assistant Fang, himself and Mr. Chen – she might be able to learn quickly. But the boss was right in one sense: Lin Yang was nothing like Berenice.

Yet a pall hung over him despite his sudden impassioned idea: it was the bald and repetitious statement from his boss that Berenice was almost certainly dead.

—⁓—

In fact, Berenice was very much alive. As if to reflect her elation, the sun had burst through the Beijing grey and was flooding her tiny flat, making it seem much bigger and more beautiful. Despite her late night she felt almost light-headed and rose at just after nine, made herself a cup of tea and mused about the previous night. She had taken a taxi home at five o'clock in the morning as George had to work early and she did not want to trouble him more; he had opened a huge vista of life to her and she had no intention of impressing herself on him too much early on. That would come later. Men did not like to feel trapped – she knew that. Later on, when they met again, her plan – conceived without thinking yet inherently formed – would be put into action. Yet she had to be subtle: he was far more worldly and intelligent than Shuo and, yes, experienced in the ways of the world. She admonished herself for being calculating yet conciliated herself with the fact that all women had to be thus these days or they wouldn't get on. After all, she had been doing it at work all her life. It just wasn't the same when applied to romance. Or love. Love? That word had popped into her mind without any provocation and she trembled a moment before telling herself that these were early days – early day, even – and she should not expect more than could be achieved carefully and slowly over time. There was still so much to know about George: was he really as wonderful as he seemed? What secrets did he have? Would she mind if he did? Was he married? Well, that was doomed from the start, she decided. If all went as well as she hoped then that would not last much longer! Then she felt ashamed at her thoughts and again admonished herself for being cruel: his wife – if he had one – was entitled to him more than she was. They may even have children, who would also have something to say, for they were bound to be at least in their teens or early twenties. She speculated about George's age: again, in the whirlwind of the evening, it was something that had not been touched upon – all the other things they discussed and laughed about seemed to make that question so much less important.

He had suggested she come and see one of his TV programmes being made and had said there would be one next week. Next week! That seemed an eternity away. Thank goodness she would see him again this evening. Well, if there was a mistress around, then she had already been given the push!

She had thought of going back to work but now she would take the time off she was owed. She would get back in touch with the office next week. Until then, her whole world focus was George. And she was already loving that prospect.

Chapter Eleven

—◦◦◦—

"Hi, Yang, it's me."

"Hi, sexy!"

Shuo felt boosted by the description. No-one had ever called him that before and his mobile seemed to glow brighter as she said it. He did, too, with that sensuous feeling in his loins that makes life worthwhile. Indeed, the whole purpose of life: sex. Lust. Procreation. The animals did it and we are animals. Or were, until we assumed this supposed veneer of sophistication, which had led to the rape of the planet, pollution, greed... and the inevitable consequence of that sexual urge – overpopulation. Yet here he was almost instinctively wanting to give Lin Yang a child. Reason versus desire – the human contradiction. "Thanks, babe," he replied. "How are you?"

"Better since I met you."

"I'm at work so can't talk too much; but I might have something that interests you."

"You showed me that last night."

Shuo blushed. Just for once – and particularly at this

precise moment – he wished she wasn't being so skittish. "Stop it – this is important. Tell me – what exactly is it that you do? For a job? I mean, I know you're a graphics designer for a news channel, but what does that actually *mean*?"

"I don't want to talk about work. I want to talk about you."

"Yes, yes. But, please: what is it you actually *do*?"

She suddenly realised the urgency in his voice. "Well, I create captions and pictures – little videos and animations, too, sometimes – to illustrate the online news. And design the colours and mood to match the stories – a bit like wearing the right clothes for the right event, if you like: that's an image you'll understand in your business. But I do it all on a computer – I'm a sort of graphic artist, I envisage things."

"Have you ever done fashion?"

"Yeah, once or twice, when I first started. I used to design my own clothes before I got this job. They weren't very good, but… Why are you asking me all this?"

"I can't go into that now. But if you want it, I might have a job for you. Permanent, well-paid. With me, in my company."

"With you? That would be nice. Why?"

Shuo paused: this was the tricky bit. "The girl I was working with has… well, it looks as though she's been killed in an air crash."

"Not Chengdu?"

"Yes. Possibly. It hasn't been confirmed yet, but…"

"Oh, my goodness – how awful. Was it the girl I saw you with when I came to your office?"

Shuo hadn't realised she had seen Berenice on that day and was blindsided for a moment. Then, evasively, he replied, "It might have been."

"You looked very fond of her."

"Er, well, she was very nice."

"Beautiful, too."

"Yes, she is – was. But might you be interested?"

There was a pause. "Of course."

"Can you get your CV to me as soon as possible?"

"Ye-es…"

"Great. Emphasise the fashion bit – you know, make it sound even more than it is really. Well, not too much – but what you're comfortable with. And don't tell the head of your department, just in case."

"*I'm* the head of my department. I *am* my department! There's only four of us here." She laughed. "Don't you listen to anything I tell you?"

"Oh… sorry. You distract me too much."

She giggled. That lovely giggle. Berenice seldom laughed out loud. Or giggled. Never, actually. Always controlled. "And I've always wanted to work for a bigger company." This was said *sotto voce*.

"Well, now's your chance. Get the CV to me as soon as you can – but make it good."

"Of course it'll be good. I *am* good."

"You don't need to tell me that." It was his turn to be saucy.

"I know. See you tonight?"

"You bet. Bye."

Shuo rang off. He was excited – Lin Yang might soon be working with him. He was excited in another way, too. Lin Yang did that to him.

—⁓—

'Unknown'. That's what it said on her phone as it rang. *It must be George*, she thought. Had she given him her number? Of course she had: how can you keep in touch without a number? Or was it Shuo trying to catch her out by hiding his? She dithered a moment: well, if it was Shuo, she would just have to tell him. And that was that. She pressed 'answer' and put the phone to her ear. The voice instantly calmed her – enveloped her, even, with its warm and comforting tones. How different voices sounded on a phone – one could hear every nuance, every movement of the vocal cords, every syllable so much more clearly. She felt consumed by it, inspired, exhilarated.

"Hello, is that Berenice?" the voice said.

Their first phone call! "Hello," she said, annoyed that there was a tremble in her voice.

"It's George."

"Yes, I know. I recognised your voice."

"Good."

"I love your voice."

There was a pause at the other end. "Thank you. I love yours, too." Another pause, then: "Well, now we have each other's numbers there's no stopping us, is there?"

"I hope not," she replied, a little too hastily.

He laughed. That rich, resonant, creamy laugh. "I can't talk for long as I'll be rehearsing and then recording a show soon so I might not be able contact you. But I just wanted to say 'Hi' and hope you're feeling OK."

"Yes, very much so." She almost dreaded asking the next obvious pleasantry in case he had changed his mind but nevertheless continued: "And you?"

The hush made her heart sink for an instant before his answer came: "Never felt so wonderful in my life." There was an even longer hush as neither quite then knew what to say next. Eventually, she managed to squeeze out, "I'm so pleased."

"This is serious," he said eventually.

Whether he meant it or not, Berenice was not going to let the moment pass; so she confirmed it by saying, softly but emphatically, "I know."

After a moment, he responded, "I haven't felt like this for years. You're an extraordinary woman. I never thought I'd feel tongue-tied with you but… there's so much I want to say that I don't know where to start."

"That's exactly how I feel, too."

"Can't wait to see you again."

"Nor me, you. Tonight?"

"Er, of course. If you'd *like* to."

That famous English reserve, she thought, *with the emphasis on the word 'like'*. "Of course I want to – it was me who just suggested it." With that, they both started laughing.

When they stopped, he continued, "God, you're amazing. Look, I can come to your flat if you're open to that. I'd love to see where you live. Helps me understand the person better."

She was wary of this comment – he'd done this before. Then thought, *Of course he has; he's much older than I am.* She continued: "It's very small. Not as big as your flat. But you're welcome to come round. I'll prepare a meal for you."

"That sounds wonderful. How could I ever resist?"

"I'll text you my address. What time do you want to come over?"

"Now." She was surprised but tingled at the prospect; he quickly went on: "But I can't, sadly. Around seven is the soonest I could get there – or is even that too early?"

Seven? She had to clean and tidy the flat, go out and get the meal, prepare it… "No, not too early at all. As soon as you like." There was another hesitation as if they were both careering along in a car where the brakes had failed, were about to hit a brick wall and just couldn't stop. Yet neither seemed to care: they seemed to be together, even if apart.

"See you later, then. Don't forget to text me your address."

"I'll do that now." They rang off. She texted her address immediately and then went to sit down for a moment. She felt weak with excitement and anticipation.

—◊—

It was early afternoon when the CV from Lin Yang came through to Shuo's office. It was concise but fuller than he had imagined. She was almost the same age as he was, which surprised him: he had perceived her to be somewhat younger. Yet what she had written was superb; she had cleverly used her experience to date to give a perfect picture of what Shuo thought his boss was after, even if her business was different to his and Berenice's. But that was less important than its sense of purpose and confidence: perhaps she was better suited to the position than he had really thought. And he felt guilty that she had obviously taken in all that he had said to her, whereas he had been so one-tracked that he had either not listened or – if he had – forgotten much that she had told him. He made one or two tweaks to the document – her grammar was not as good as his – and printed it off. He read it again and honestly thought she would stand a good chance, especially if Mr. Chen met her in person. That was the difficult bit.

He put it in an envelope, sealed it, and walked up to his office; seeing Mr. Chen had someone with him, he left the document with his assistant who was in her position and not off prowling around the building annoying people. Aggressively, she asked, "What's this?"

"Mr. Chen's expecting it from me. Please give it to him as soon as you can, if you would."

Natalya glowered at him: she always did, which was why Shuo – and just about everyone else, for that matter – tried to have the shortest engagement with her possible. She was not the nicest of people and seemed to exude an invisible cloud of ethereal repellence. She always rather resented being asked to do things, even when part of her job – it was beneath her; indeed, she felt she should not only be running Mr. Chen's department but the whole organisation – and even China itself, probably. Politically motivated, she was the daughter of a high-level Soviet *apparatchik* and had originally come to Beijing from Moscow in the '80s when a youngster and the countries had had a sort of *entente cordiale*; she had wanted to help the Mother country appropriate China, but she arrived just before *glasnos*t happened and she wasn't allowed back, whereupon the Berlin Wall – and Soviet Communism – collapsed. And she had bemoaned all three events ever since.

"I'll see what I can do," she said curtly, as if it was a huge favour. Shuo left: there were so many more pleasant people in the building than her...

He went back to his office and tried to concentrate; his pulse rate was up as he couldn't stop thinking of Lin Yang working in the same building as him. Just as he had originally felt when he started going out with Berenice. He sighed: was he lucky to have met someone at a critical juncture just after his first love had disappeared, or would it all go sour and he would miss Berenice even more?

The answer to that would become chillingly apparent in due course.

Chapter Twelve

—◊—

It was mid-afternoon and George stood at the back of the control room, observing the recording of his television show. The banks of monitors, the director's barked instructions and the calm but authoritative tones of the production assistant, along with the hysterical laughter of a technologically-augmented audience, still absorbed and thrilled him, even after all these years. It was the same feeling, whether in Beijing or London: the language difference made little impact on the overall exuberance of the televisual experience – it was a heady and compelling emotion. Yet, on all the many monitors in front of him, each displaying a different feed – cameras, graphics, prompting scripts and more – he could see only one picture: the face of Berenice. On every one it seemed to be there, sweetly smiling and making his pulse race.

Yet just before the show had begun, he had received an email from his wife back in England, which had put him in a bad mood as she was being silly, in his view, and was also disturbing his reverie. They had agreed to split up many weeks ago and, although it had made him happy at the time, it had also depressed him. Yet his return to Beijing had been portentous: the company had asked for more shows and offered him a luxury all-expenses-paid flat not far from the studios in San Li Tun; he had spent the last six weeks adapting and setting up a series, a gameshow he had created in London and sold to the ITV network, and then it had been franchised to a Beijing station and here he was, in his element, feted by all and regarded as a god by all and sundry – especially the beautiful Chinese girls, who smiled and giggled as they passed him. He was seen as a '*shry-ger*' – a handsome man – by many of them and had felt he might soon have to start fighting them off, especially if they had known he was thinking of getting divorced.

And then he had met Berenice. Not only beautiful but highly intelligent, cultured, beautifully dressed and worldly. He just could not wait to see her again, to caress her olivy, smooth skin and smell her wonderful aroma, which was completely unlike any girl's he had ever inhaled before. On top of that, she used a subtle but arousing perfume, yet he had realised that even when she had washed that off in the shower, before she had left, her own scent had replaced it, just as bewitchingly, so there was always one or the other to look forward to.

He was suddenly aware of his phone buzzing in his jacket pocket, which he had taken a moment to acknowledge, being consumed by the noise of the programme – and his dislocation somewhere in the heavens as he thought of Berenice. He took the phone out and opened it – it was her! He could see the picture he had taken of her when she was asleep that morning; it was obvious she was naked, yet it was completely decent and it showed her satisfied face with a slight hint of a smile, rather like the *Mona Lisa*, bathed in the soft light of early morning. He pressed 'answer' and quickly left the control room so he could hear her dulcet voice.

Once outside, he just said, "Hello, darling." He had not called her that before, and he wondered suddenly if he had sounded too forward, expectant.

There was a tiny pause, and then she said, "George?" as if questioning whether she had got the right man.

'*Damn*,' he thought; so he added, "Hello, Berenice."

His senses were then soothed when she replied, "Ah, it *is* you."

"It most certainly is. Er, how are you?"

"I wondered if you'd recognised my voice."

"Of course – and I could see your picture, too."

"What picture?"

Damn again – she hadn't known, of course. "Er, I took one of you this morning while you were asleep."

"Naughty boy... Is it decent?"

He could hear she was stifling a giggle. "Of course – I would never demean you."

"I know. I hope we're still meeting tonight?"

"I thought we'd already arranged that."

"Yes, we did; I just wanted to hear your voice again to make sure I wasn't dreaming."

"No, you weren't. And nor was I. You bet we're meeting tonight."

"Same arrangements we discussed earlier?"

"Absolutely."

"Can't wait." There was a pause; he hoped she would say the magic word, 'darling', but it was not forthcoming, so he said, "Sorry, I hope you didn't mind my calling you 'darling' a moment ago – I just couldn't help it."

"Not at all." Still no hint of its being proffered, though; he wasn't sure whether she was playing with him, holding back the word for a heightened effect when it came... or she just didn't feel confident – or sure enough – to use it yet. Oh, well; he would just have to hope that she'd get over her reluctance later tonight. "Well, I must go... I'm in the middle of a show... so, see you later. Seven o'clock at yours."

"Yes. Can't wait. Darling." And she immediately rang off.

Suddenly, George was on another planetary dimension. She said it! And he swiftly had to find a chair lest his trembling knees crumbled with emotion. Now he *knew* he was hopelessly in love with her – already.

Berenice stayed looking at her phone for a few moments and smiled with a happy satisfaction. It was not one of triumph or where she felt she was scoring points, just carefully ensuring that there was still mystique in her, which she hoped would take a lifetime to discover fully. She was already in love, too.

—m—

The phone on Shuo's desk rang: it was Mr. Chen. "Your friend's CV looks hopeful," he said. "Do you want to ask her to ring me to make an appointment?"

"Of course, sir. Thank you. I'll do it now." He put the phone down and immediately rang Lin Yang on her mobile. When she answered he burst straight in and proclaimed, "Well done – my boss wants you to call him and fix an interview."

"Oh, great. Er… now?"

"Why not?"

"OK – it's a good moment for me. Two of my colleagues are out the office so it's quite empty. Anything I should know first?"

"Yes; you'll probably be answered by a dragon called Natalya, his PA.

"A Chinese dragon?" she quipped.

"No – a Russian one."

"A bear, then?"

"Ha-ha! Yes, very funny – a bear. But be very careful, don't get angry – she'll try to stop you seeing him – just be patient and say Mr. Chen has asked you to call him until she puts you through."

"All right."

"Good luck – and let me know what happens. Bye."

"Bye."

He was suddenly aware of a dark shadow behind him, which seemed to invade his space and cause interference with his soul. He turned round on his chair to see that it was Natalya. "I heard that," she said venomously, and swiftly, purposefully, walked out. *Oh no*, Shuo thought: and hoped that Lin was ringing that second before Natalya got back to her office.

A few minutes later, Lin Yang returned his call. "I've got an interview next week – Monday," she said in hushed tones – there must now have been someone close to her in the office.

"Great – so you must have avoided Natalya," as he furtively looked around to ensure she wasn't behind him again.

"Yes – got straight through. Mr. Chen seems nice enough."

Seeing that the woman in question wasn't there, Shuo continued, "Yes, he is… and you were lucky – she heard what I just said about her to you! She'll hate you on sight when you come in, now – although she would have done anyway because you're so beautiful." There was a pause. "Thanks, handsome – and I'll bear that in mind. Thanks for everything – must go. Work. See you later."

"Yup – bye."

Shuo sat back and contemplated things. Perhaps she *was* even more capable than Berenice… certainly cannier. Fun, infectious. Despite Berenice's attributes, there was a coldness there: she had always lacked warmth. Perhaps Lin Yang's abundance of it would soon more than make up for that. At this precise moment, he was increasingly sure that it would…

Chapter Thirteen

—◊—

George's involvement in the recording finished an hour or so after his talk with Berenice, so he went home, showered and changed into his smartest casual clothes. He shaved again, too, to ensure he wouldn't feel like a cheese grater on Berenice's beautifully soft cheeks, and finished off with a subtle but long-lasting – and ridiculously expensive – aftershave.

He looked at the result in the mirror – not bad for fifty. But how old was she? They had talked so extensively about so much else – tastes, prejudices, pet hates, music, poetry, literature, to name but a few – that age had not crept into the conversation. Or perhaps he had just not dared. Perhaps she had not dared, either... He thought Berenice must be around twenty-five to thirty and grimaced at himself; was he cradle-snatching? A difference of around twenty-five years... just about acceptable. He thought of his friend Alessandro who had spent almost a lifetime with his second wife, marrying a girl twenty-seven years younger than he. And it was still working beautifully. It was good to have yardsticks like that... Berenice could be older, of course – just beautifully preserved and well-dressed, which made things even better. He mused that, generally, Chinese girls dressed nowhere as well as Japanese girls: the latter had more discreet taste. But it only underlined the fact that Berenice *did* have that dress sense and along with everything else it was that which made her perfect. To him, anyway. And now it was time to go to see her. A shudder of anticipatory pleasure ran through his body and it helped propel him through the door.

—◊—

A little earlier that same evening, Shuo and Lin Yang had decided to go shopping. It was a chilly evening and the plethora of malls in her district exuded an allure as a result – they were warm, bright and distracting. She had dressed more casually for this evening in tight jeans, sparkly trainers and a loose top boasting the legend 'Fun Girl'. For his part, Shuo had dressed more traditionally than before as he wanted to project a sense of authority; after all, they were possibly going to be working together after next week and she had to realise he was the boss. Berenice had always assumed the mantle of boss before, but now the emphasis could change. He was beginning to feel rather smug about his hopeful ability to take on his second *protégée*, but this one would be in hock to *him*. That was how it had supposed to be with Berenice, but her innate superiority in everything had made him the junior partner in both their work and amorous lives. So he was glad Yang had dressed in a more girly fashion – it was a good result for him. Or so he thought: Yang, of course, had done this for exactly that purpose. Canny and clever... Shuo was already the junior partner, but she was astute enough to make him believe the opposite.

In fact, she knew she had him around her little finger already.

After a while, they found themselves hovering around a perfumery area where Lin Yang implied she would like to try a new fragrance. Loving the fact that Berenice had always smelled gorgeous, Shuo was quick to agree. Yang always wore some lovely aromas too, but even he knew that it was nice to have different perfumes for various occasions so did not demur.

Also at the counter was a well-dressed older man – Western – trying to ascertain the best perfume for his new partner, his basic Mandarin cutting little ice with the bored girl at the counter. On an impulse, Yang walked up to the man and offered to help, in English, for which he was most gracious, and accepted. Her grasp of the language – albeit somewhat hesitant – was nevertheless adequate enough to assist; yet the discovery of this talent astonished Shuo, who had not hitherto known she was capable of speaking English at all. He was impressed: were there no limits to this amazing girl? Shuo wandered a little distance away and started sampling some fragrances which took his eye: one of them, 'Heavenly Scent', attracted him but he realised with a shudder that he recognised the smell – it was the one Berenice had usually worn. He put it back quickly and wandered back to where Yang and the man were in animated, if limited, conversation. *Damn 'gweilos'*, he thought. *Always after our beautiful Chinese women.*

Yang turned to Shuo and said, "I think this is nice – what do you think?" It was Heavenly Scent. He tried to distance himself from agreeing it was nice, but Yang was resolute. "I really like it," she announced, and, turning to the man, said, "and I think your lady will love it, too." Shuo was horrified – he did *not* want Yang to have the same perfume as Berenice!

The man looked at her and said, "I think you're right – thank you so much for your help; you're very kind." With that, he bought the bottle, which was put in a little purple bag, thanked Yang profusely for her help and walked away.

She looked at Shuo and said, "What a nice man. Class." She looked at another bottle of perfume, which Shuo hoped to God – *please* – she would prefer. But no; she wanted Heavenly Scent too. Shuo paid, Yang kissed and thanked him profusely, and they eventually meandered back to her flat. Shuo consoled himself with the fact that the perfume would smell very different on her to Berenice. At least, he hoped so.

—※—

When he arrived at Berenice's flat, George was flummoxed as to whether he had the correct tower: they all seemed identical, in true Chinese fashion. He hesitated, his finger hovering over the bell: if this was the wrong block then it would be difficult to explain to a possibly angry resident in his sketchy Mandarin that he had the wrong flat. As if a wish in a dream which miraculously comes true, he hoped that she would have seen him... and suddenly, the door opened and she was standing there. Slightly taken aback with surprise and relief, he almost dropped the flowers, bottle of wine and the little purple bag with the perfume in it, her expectant look and limpid eyes piercing his soul like arrows.

"Hello, George; I was looking out for you. People always have difficulty finding this the first time."

George was speechless – her beauty was even deeper than he had remembered just a few hours before, and he suddenly felt like a tongue-tied, gauche teenager. And that had not happened for years. Many years.

"Are you coming in?" she asked with a querulous tremble in her voice.

"Ah, yes, yes… of course I am! Dear Berenice – lovely to see you. So pleased you were waiting for me." And he pecked her cheek as his arms flailed about while trying to imply the huge number of flats.

She looked at him with what appeared to be a cheeky smile dancing on her lips and held the door open for him.

As he entered, he felt out of control. Yet it did not worry him – not a bit of it: he just knew he was going to enjoy the evening, almost whatever course it took.

When they arrived at the twentieth floor, it took a moment to realise the lift doors had opened: they had been lucky in that no-one was in there with them and their kiss had seemed like a timeless elevation to heaven. Slightly dishevelled, they left the confines of its embrace and she guided him to her flat opposite.

"Hello, darling," she said, and again kissed him ravenously as her front door closed behind them. She had cooked a special meal and the table was beautifully laid; she took the flowers from him and put them in a vase already filled with water in the centre of the table. She just knew he would bring flowers!

"Ah, Heavenly Scent," she proclaimed, opening the little purple bag. "My favourite perfume! How did you know?"

"Er, I didn't, I... just thought it would smell great on you."

Such synergy they had! The table was then by-passed as she guided him down the tiny hall to her bedroom. "Don't worry, the meal will keep for as long as necessary," she mumbled as she tore off his jacket. In his ecstasy of emotion, George still managed to notice a bottle of chilling champagne in an ice bucket on the bedside table. *My goodness*, he thought, *she's got everything...* Yet it was some time before the champagne was drunk. And much later still that the meal was consumed.

—⁓—

The man rolled over in bed and suddenly realised he felt unwell: his chest was tight and becoming more so, and a small pain was rapidly becoming bigger. He felt dizzy as he sat up and took a slug of water from the glass beside his bed. No difference. He stumbled out of his filthy bed and tried to make it to the phone in the hall to ring for an ambulance, but the response took so long that he was dead before the health service answered. After a few hours, the police broke into his flat and found him lying on the floor with his hands clutching his chest and the phone at his ear.

Chapter Fourteen

—ɷ—

Berenice's mother took the news with a shrug of the shoulder and a dismissive, "OK." She put the phone down and secretly felt glad that her husband's brother was no more. She had reluctantly admitted to herself many years ago that he was a monster who had defiled her beautiful daughter; yet in those days, before China opened up to the world, ignoring it was her best chance of survival: keep your head down, say nothing, admit nothing. She had turned a blind eye to him, which was why her relationship with her daughter had become so tenuous – distant, even – to the point of disappearance. Despite a desire to know what Berenice was doing – that she was in Beijing was all she really knew, working for some fancy Western firm – she had resisted any contact because she knew Berenice would never forgive her. And rightly so, she sighed: but Berenice had to be told. It was a mother's duty to do so – if only to let her know that the tormenting demon was finally gone. It was Saturday morning, so Berenice would be at home; she looked up her daughter's number in an old and dog-eared little book and cautiously dialled it.

In her flat, Berenice could hear the phone ringing in the hall but found the unclothed George draped around her, and it was difficult to move without waking him. Yet none of her few friends rang on her landline phone: she had often thought of cancelling it but knew some relatives might only have that number, so – out of duty rather than desire – had decided to keep it. Therefore, it must be a relative… Perhaps her mother had passed on: she had better go and get it. She roughly pushed George away, who turned over and went back to sleep as she ran naked into the hall.

When almost there, the ringing stopped. She grasped the receiver and held it to her ear, but the line was already dead. With a feeling of dread, mitigated by the fact that George was there into whose arms she could throw herself if she needed to (any excuse would do – even the death of her mother!) – she decided to call her. She had not spoken to her for many years but instinctively she felt she should try. She went back to the bedroom and put on her bra and knickers: even though her mother would not be able to see her, she felt she had to be 'decently' dressed. George was still asleep and snoring lightly, so she added a dressing-gown to her attire and went back to the phone. She looked up the number, dialled it and waited.

In her mother's hallway in her tiny flat in Chengdu, the phone was making a noise. She stepped over to it and cautiously picked it up.

"Mother?" a distant younger female voice enquired.

A wave of guilty love surged down the line, yet all she could manage in that millisecond of emotion was, "Yes."

"It's me, your daughter. Berenice."

"Yes, I recognised your voice." There was a pause, as each wondered what to say next.

"Did you just call me?"

"Yes." There was a pause. Then: "Your uncle's dead."

"Oh." As far as she was concerned, he had been dead ever since she had at last managed to get away from him. But now it was, apparently, official.

"I'm sorry to tell you this."

"To be honest, I'm delighted."

"Yes, I thought you might be. So am I, if the truth be known." There was a pause, then she continued: "What he did to you was unforgiveable."

Now it was Berenice's turn to be surprised. "You knew?"

"Yes, my dear – I'm so sorry…" She started to weep. "But things were so different then and he had a hold over me like he did over you. He was the most repellent man I ever met."

Berenice could feel tears welling up inside her as well, but she would control them – like she had on so many occasions all those years ago; yet this time they were more from compassion than fear.

Her mother continued: "I don't know when the funeral is because I haven't had a chance to organise it yet. But I'll let you know."

"No need – I won't go to it."

"No – of course not. Nor will I, probably." And she started to laugh, as if a huge burden had suddenly been lifted. Berenice started to laugh, too, and they both spent a few moments doing so. Then it went quiet and her mother said quietly, "I'd like to see you again. And I don't know if I can cope with organising your uncle's funeral on my own—"

"We'll see." There was a silence: years of being ignored by her mother could not wash away that feeling of indifference so easily. "I'll get back to you soon. There's lots to tell you, but this is not a good moment." She paused, then: "But what you should know, Mother, is that I've met a wonderful man and I'm hopelessly in love." Not wishing to say more or hear her mother's response, she curtly said, "Bye," and put the phone down. Then she just stared at it in contemplation of what had just happened.

In the bedroom, George had been woken by the laughter and heard the last thing Berenice said. He had never felt so happy in his life.

—⁂—

It was Monday morning and Shuo was looking forward to the arrival of Lin Yang at the office. Ten o'clock; it was now nine forty-seven. He was trembling a little and his hands were sweaty, which meant he had dropped his pen a few times and his phone once. He had been detailed to go and get her at the prescribed time and guide her past the fiendish Natalya. Then he would go and have a glass of tea and try to relax while he waited for her.

At the same time, Berenice had decided to see her mother after all in Chengdu: she had to help her organise the funeral and – having told work anyway that she was taking the holiday due to her – had not bothered to inform anyone. She was enjoying the freedom of being away from the office and not pretending she and Shuo were not having a relationship, and any lingering doubts now about the cessation of it had been completely destroyed by her all-consuming relationship with George. This gave her a sense of release, freedom and soaring spirits which she had never encountered in her life before; when she eventually got back to the office, things would now be so much easier. Her new situation was giving her the confidence to speak even to her mother as an equal and it was a strange sensation: indeed, she was positively looking forward to seeing her. They had not met for so long and each sensed a belated desire to rediscover each other and bury any hatchet which might have been around, which had previously so spoiled their relationship. She would ring the office later in the week and inform them she would be back at the start of the next week. She would not be in Chengdu long: and, anyway, she wanted to spend as much time with George as possible. But he was off to Shanghai for two days so it seemed a good time to see her mother in his absence. She had two days before he would be gone and they would have a wonderful weekend when he came back the following Friday. She even suspected George would arrange something special, which would give the prospect of seeing him again an added piquancy.

—ᴍ—

Shuo's desk phone rang and the receptionist informed him that a certain Lin Yang was here to see him. He thanked the lady and then informed Mr. Chen that Lin Yang had arrived: he was glad that Natalya was obviously causing trouble somewhere else in the building as he got straight through to him: Mr. Chen told Shuo to bring Lin Yang straight in. Quickly checking his attire in the glass partition, he bolted to the lift.

When he saw Lin Yang, it was as if he were seeing her for the first time again: she was even more beautiful than he had ever seen her; she was wearing high heels, a demure skirt but with a discreet slit up the side, black stockings and a white blouse which pronounced and exposed just enough of her bust to be mildly provocative but not tarty or outrageous. The ensemble was finished off by a matching suit top and a dash of colour from a magenta silk scarf around her neck which offset her features perfectly. Instantly, Shuo felt his manhood challenged as he walked as fast as he dared to meet her. With a show of fake formality, they shook hands and made small talk as they entered the lift which was, fortuitously, quite full: ruffled attire would not have been the best introduction to a potential new boss! At Mr. Chen's office, he guided Yang past the returned but disapproving Natalya and through the open door of his boss's office, smiled sweetly at the gatekeeper on his way out, and went to calm himself down with his promised glass of tea.

Berenice was looking for flights on her tablet. The usual airline she used had suspended flights to Chengdu for a few days whilst the fallout from an air crash there – which had apparently happened a few days ago and of which, in firstly her depressed mood and then her ecstatic meeting with George – she had not heard about. She tried another one and eventually booked a flight around the same time as George was leaving for his flight to Shanghai, so she could cadge a luxurious taxi drive with him to the airport! She then texted George with the news and waited only a few seconds for his reply, which just said 'Wonderful. Xx'. Elysium had hitherto been written about as a fictitious place... but she was now certain it actually existed and that she had found it...

Chapter Fifteen

—◊—

"I've been offered the job!" Yang's phone had rung just as he had returned to his office: she had been in with Mr. Chen for some time and his wait had exhausted five glasses of tea.

"Wow – that's fantastic! When do you start?"

"Monday!"

"Well done! Oh, I can't wait to have you working here with me."

"Nor me. Have you got a few minutes? We could have a quick celebratory drink. I told the office I'd be back at two. So there's time."

"Hmm. I'm a bit busy, and I should go and thank Mr. Chen and discuss what he wants you to do—"

"He's told me that already – I can tell *you*!"

"It's not as simple as that! Look, go and wait on the little seat opposite the entrance and I'll be there as soon as I can."

"OK. But be quick. I'm waiting for you." She rang off.

He paused a moment, then rang Mr. Chen's office, only to have his happiness punctured by the oppressive Natalya. "He can see you in an hour," she said sternly. "What's it about?"

"Lin Yang."

"I don't know that name."

"She's the girl who just walked past you after he interviewed her for Berenice's job."

"Oh – her." The disdain was redolent in her voice. "All right, I'll tell him. Twelve thirty. Don't be late. He's busy." And the phone went dead. He looked around: his floor was fairly empty. So he slipped out.

As she had expected, Yang observed Shuo coming out the building in about the same time she had predicted – four minutes. He guided her away from the front of the building and when they were out of its sight, she threw her arms around him and kissed him passionately, leaving red lipstick on his cheek and collar. "Let's get a drink – on me," she said excitedly, and pulled him towards the entrance of a basement food court area.

Once seated with a beer for him and a cocktail for her, she let fly. "Thank you, dear Shuo, thank you! It's going to be the best job I've ever had! And all thanks to you! And the money – it's great; almost twice as much as I'm making now." As she continued in this vein, Shuo nodded and feigned listening as her excitement washed over him and he wondered whether she was now earning more than he was. And whether she would take over his job, too, rather than the way it had been before with Berenice. Suddenly, he wondered if he had done the right thing.

If he had known what would happen next, he would have worried even more.

—⁂—

Shuo stepped into Mr. Chen's office and closed the door. He didn't want Natalya hearing any part of their conversation.

"Sit down," said Mr. Chen. Shuo did so, nervously. "You were right," he continued, "she seems a very accomplished young lady."

"Yes, I think she is," mumbled Shuo.

"So I've offered her the job on a trial basis." Yang hadn't told Shuo that bit. "I think she'll make the grade with flying colours, but one cannot be too sure these days. And Berenice is, sadly, a hard act to follow. So, she'll shadow you in your office; Fang can join you there too until Yang is up to speed. Then we'll see."

Shuo felt he had to interject: "We won't need Fang. She's nice, and helped Berenice: but I won't have any use for her."

Mr. Chen's face acquired a knowing smile as Shuo said this, surmising that Shuo did not want the pretty little Fang in his office in case it caused difficulties. Actually, Shuo just wanted to be with Lin Yang alone...

Mr. Chen returned to his business-like demeanour and continued: "All right; if that's what you want... Basically, you taught Berenice the ropes and then she went stratospheric so I can only hope Miss Lin will do the same. But if... and I don't expect this, I have to say, she proves to be a disappointment then I'll have to find someone else. But I have a hunch she'll have a bright future here. Well done for finding her."

"That's great, sir. I'm pleased, too."

"I'll bet you are," he said with a sly grin. "She's lovely. Almost as lovely as Berenice." He then clasped the bridge of his nose as if trying not to cry. "Sorry, I adored that girl... and I still haven't heard from the authorities if her body has been recovered. I don't know why they're being so obstinate. She never divulged any next of kin, either, and she left nothing on file so I don't even know where to start looking. Do you know if she has any?"

"Well, only her mother, and she had cut all contact with her as far as I could make out: something that happened when she was young, I think. She never revealed what it was to me, though. But if she's still alive I've never heard her mentioned. And I didn't even know she had the aunt in Chengdu you talked of. That was news to me, as I told you."

"Hm. Oh, well. Just teach Yang the basic ropes – where everything is, and so on, and who she should talk to when she needs help. I've given her a good salary – not as much as Berenice, of course – but it's quite generous."

Shuo was relieved about that, at least. "I think she's very happy with it," he confirmed.

"Good. Well, let's see what happens, then. Back to work."

Shuo stood up and, as he opened the door – as much to annoy Natalya as because he meant it – he said, "Thanks for giving her the opportunity. I'm sure she won't let you down, sir."

"Let's hope not." And he waved Shuo away.

Shuo could feel the laser burns in his neck as he passed through the office, but Natalya had the upper hand for a moment when she said sharply, "Get your friend to fill in these forms before Monday morning, and then give them to me, will you?" Then, more directly as Shuo turned to face her and take the documents, "I assume you are 'seeing' her, aren't you?"

Shuo said nothing, took the documents and left.

—⁂—

That evening, George surprised Berenice by taking her to a hastily-arranged music concert in the brand new Beijing Arts Centre; she had never been to a classical music venue before and, although she had always instinctively liked the sound of 'serious' music when she heard it, like many of her generation, she had let it pass as she did not 'understand' it.

"Nothing to understand," George said jauntily when she told him this. "Just enjoy it and let it enwrap you. You have deep emotions, so it will – just don't fight it."

Not long into the first movement – a Mozart piano concerto – she knew what he meant; it suddenly just made sense as it transported her into realms of consciousness she had never experienced before. She squeezed George's hand: implicitly understanding the reason for her action, he gave her an empathetic look, as if to say, "I told you so." As the music engulfed her, she realised she had met what a colleague had once termed a 'soulmate'; already knowing she loved George, this sense of complete absorption had heightened that emotion and engulfed, bewildered and drained her. Inspired her, too, for, despite feeling physically weak in his presence, she also sensed he had made her emotionally stronger – and would never be the same again.

George had comprehended this, too.

After the concert, they went to a low-lit restaurant and had an intimate meal; the waiters and waitresses seemed to know George well and this concerned her a little but, seeing the concern in her eyes as he flirted lightly with a departing waitress, he leaned forward, held her hand and looked deep into her eyes, saying, "Forgive me, I'm a flirt… but if I wasn't, then I'd never have had the guts to come and talk to you in the first place."

"But you had to – you nearly ran me over!"

He paused, and leaned even closer. "Some would not have done; they'd have made sure you were OK and then driven off."

Berenice looked back at him even more deeply and cautiously enquired, "Really?"

"Dearest – darling – Berenice. In less than two days you have bewitched and conquered me. Now, I just have real interest for only one girl in the world... and I'm looking at her."

Berenice leaned the final two inches between them and kissed his lips; a thrill ran through her body and stimulated her vagina so much that she gasped as she experienced a small but intense orgasm. That had never happened to her before. What was this man doing to her? Well, whatever it was, she never wanted it to end. "I think I'm in love with you," she said tremulously, massaging his cheek between her thumb and forefinger, her bright painted nails and olive skin contrasting with the more rugged and slightly wrinkled face of her friend.

"I *know* I'm in love with you," he replied.

Chapter Sixteen

—〰—

The next two days passed normally for both couples; Lin Yang was so excited about her new situation working with Shuo that she could neither talk nor think of much else. She had asked permission of her boss to let her go early by taking holiday she had accumulated and not used because she had enjoyed her job so much. So if she had any reservations about leaving it, this was more to do with suddenly working at a huge, international company rather than the small, friendly and intimate one she was used to. Yet the challenge, greater responsibility and much larger salary made her determined to succeed in her new surroundings. There was a steel in her now, which Shuo found sexually exciting – as long as it did not become too dominant: one of the reasons he liked her was because she was compliant…

As for George and Berenice, on the Wednesday morning they took a taxi from his apartment to Capital Airport, from where he flew to Shanghai and she to Chengdu.

—〰—

Her mother seemed smaller, less attractive and more ordinary than Berenice remembered from all those years ago since they had parted. And more timid than the confident dentist she had known then – she was almost reclusive now outside her circle of mah-jong friends. She welcomed Berenice warmly enough, though, and seemed genuinely flattered by the gifts Berenice had bought for her at the airport. They sat and talked for some hours after they had shared some tea and a few of the traditional Beijing Daoxiangcun cakes Berenice had brought from the capital. They then made a list of the people to inform regarding the death of her uncle and his impending funeral, and Berenice got on with that, too; soon, she had organised it for a few days hence. They had been fortunate in that there had been a space in the never-ending cycle of death and cremation in Chengdu and it was all arranged by the end of the afternoon. She would not go to the funeral, as she was adamant she wanted to get back to George, but felt glad she had managed to set things up for her mother.

Feeling tired and emotional, Berenice insisted that they went out to a restaurant that evening – on her – which seemed to trouble her mother as she would have to get ready, change and so on; but Berenice wanted to get out of the small flat, which brought back so many horrible memories for her. She knew she would have to sleep in the bedroom where her uncle had molested her but, thanks to the thought of George waiting to see her on Friday, she felt she could cope. It would be difficult but necessary.

Her mother eventually – reluctantly – agreed to go out and soon they were in a local restaurant where the advances in convivial atmosphere redolent of Beijing had yet to catch up. It was not as bright and stark as many, and there were some booths where there was a semblance of privacy, but her mother assured her the food was good so Berenice did not take any further issue. She had managed to get out of the flat into a public space and that was a relief enough in itself.

"You look well," her mother observed. "Successful."

"I'm doing well. I've taken some holiday because I broke up with a boyfriend last week."

"Oh, dear. Was he nice?" Berenice was stumped for a moment: no-one had asked her that before. The people at work either did or did not know that she and Shuo had been an item or, with her having no close friends, it had never been discussed anyway.

She hesitated for a moment, then the words, "Yes, I think so…" came out somewhat oddly.

"You must have known," her mother commented wryly.

"Well… he got me my job, and he's a nice boy—"

"Boy? How old is he?"

"Well, older than I am, but he… just seemed like a boy to me. Well, he does now, anyway."

"Go on."

"Yes, I was upset, but… then something better happened." Her mother implied with her eyes that she should continue. "Well, I've met a nice man. More suitable, very successful and… older."

"How much older?"

"About twenty-two years."

Her mother looked incredulous and blew through her teeth. "That's too much," she proclaimed.

"Not really," Berenice parried defensively. "We have a lot in common and he's already introduced me to extraordinary new things. He's literate and loves poetry, novels, writing; and music, art. He's amazing."

Her mother looked at her quizzically. "You were never interested in those things before…"

"I think that's my point."

A part of their order arrived, which stopped the interrogation for a moment; but when the waiter had disappeared her mother – having had a chance to get the bit properly between her teeth – launched forth. "That's typical of you, Berenice. Out of one bad situation and into another – too young, then too old. You join a fashion company when you should have been like me or your father and gone into medicine or teaching… What else is there about this man you've now flitted to?"

"He's English."

"English? A white ghost? What's wrong with a nice Chinese man?"

"It's not through lack of trying to find someone Chinese I can engage with, Mother; it's who you meet and under what circumstances. He's different, worldly, cultured—"

"And too old. Just think – when he's in his seventies you'll still only be in your forties. It's disgusting."

It was an issue that Berenice had thought of when she first realised her feelings for George, but whether her mother had a point or not, she wasn't going to let her get away with it. So she looked her fully in the face and just stated firmly, "Well, I love him." Despite staying outwardly calm, Berenice was really beginning to get annoyed at her mother's reaction: she had not met George, so how could she make a judgement?

"How long have you known him?"

"About five days."

"Five days?" she almost spat at her. "You can't get to know whether you love someone in five days! Your father and I took five *years* to get married."

"Well, if I waited as long as you did he'd be even older."

She looked angry and indignant: "You're not going to marry him, are you?"

Berenice looked at the paper napkin she had been nervously folding into several conflicting and arbitrary shapes as she pondered her answer. Then: "I think I'd like to, yes."

Her mother was puce with anger and frustration. "Didn't that vile uncle of yours put you off older men forever?" she demanded.

"He put me off men, full stop. Then I met Shuo, who was really nice and we had a good relationship; but there was something missing... and I couldn't have sex with him—"

"I should hope not! You should be married for that sort of carrying on."

"—but that was because of Uncle's legacy; he just put me off and poor Shuo was the casualty. But... then I met George."

"Is that someone else? Or is this the older man?"

"The older man. Look, Mother, he's completely different to either Uncle or Shuo. But perhaps deep down, I feel attracted to older men as a result of Father. And even, perversely, Uncle, even if I hated him for what he did to me. I was very young, remember – it was disgusting. And you never tried to stop him – even though you've now admitted you *knew* about what he was doing to me."

"There was nothing I could do. I needed him. He was a high-level official, who could get me things. And your father was away..."

Suddenly, it was Berenice's turn to be angry. With that offhand statement, a penny had just dropped. "Were you having sex with him, too?" she said loudly. Some people in the restaurant looked round as she said this.

"Keep your voice down," she hissed. "I know people here." Then, more quietly as the hubbub rose again: "As I said, your father was away. A woman needs things."

"Perhaps that's why I like older men after all, then," Berenice said; "I learned it from you."

Her mother reddened even more at this, and a band of perspiration stood on her forehead. "But he wasn't twenty-two years older than me – only twelve."

Berenice was brutally being reminded of why she had not seen her mother for so many years... And she was missing George.

—∿—

At the same time, in Shanghai, George was on the phone and having a similar conversation with another woman, although the invective was more measured, controlled and imbued with the cloak of boredom. They had been here before. "Well, whatever *you* think, I wish to marry her, Clarissa, if she'll accept. You should be glad – now you have a chance to *really* hate me... and you can finally make it right with Roger, or whatever his name is, without feeling guilty about the neighbours – or me – supposedly knowing. We've been apart for years – virtually divorced, in fact, anyway – so you should be glad for me as I will be for you. Just accept it."

He switched off the phone, threw it angrily on the hotel bed and strolled to the window. In the distance, the lights on the other side of the Bund and across the Yangtze River in Pudong were twinkling a fairy-like backdrop. Yet the only image he could see, framed by the sparkling haze, was Berenice's smiling face.

How he was missing her.

—⁓—

The next day, after a sleepless night being disturbed by the thoughts of what had happened so many years ago in the very bed she was now sleeping in, Berenice decided that a day out seeing attractions – or was it 'distractions'? – in the city of Chengdu was the best way to offset her mother's foul mood. And hers. She made the proposal after breakfast and her mother shrugged in a more positive than negative way. As her mother had no car, and feeling optimistic about the future after a late call from George the night before (while her mother had looked on sullenly, even more agitated as she did not speak any English), she called a taxi to take them to the Dujiangyan Irrigation System, a marvel of ancient engineering which she had last seen as a child. Then they would make a trip to Mount Qingcheng, one of the main birthplaces of Taoism. Although she and her mother would have to sit together on the journeys, they could look in different directions out of the windows and – if she was lucky – Berenice could make conversation with the taxi driver. Anything was better than talking to her mother at this moment.

They were soon out of the flat and on their way. The weather was benign and the driver talkative, so there was little chance of maternal torment, and the journey passed quickly. The ancient irrigation systems were extraordinary and meant much more to Berenice now as an adult than they had ever done when she last went as a child; her mother looked at them again cursorily, probably wishing that Berenice was not there and that she could be playing mah-jong and eating out with her friends. But for Berenice, it was like seeing her hometown anew through fresh eyes; it had certainly become more industrialised, commercial and richer than when she had left it, but parts still had a traditional Chinese charm despite the brutality of the modern architecture and the proliferation of American fast-food outlets…

Having finished their tour, Berenice managed a few less hostile words with her mother over lunch in the ancient quarter and then she hired another taxi – over her mobile phone, which impressed her mother greatly – and they were on their way to the Jianfu Palace at the top of Mount Qingcheng.

It was then that the tragedy happened.

Her mother had not looked after her health over the years and it was soon apparent that she was struggling with the steep gradients on the walkways and stairs in and to the buildings. Berenice, absorbed with the place – which she vowed in her mind she would bring George to if he ever came to meet her mother – had allowed her to fall behind and had not realised how far away she was. It was only when she started to hear shouts and wails that she stopped and turned around – to see her mother about seventy feet away, collapsed on the gravel path.

Already, a young, good-looking Chinese man was attending to her and, as she ran back to see what had happened, it was instantly obvious that she was having a heart attack. The young man was a doctor and was pumping her chest as well as occasionally giving her mouth-to-mouth resuscitation… but it was eventually without effect and her mother's head lolled back in the final move into death. Berenice burst into tears – less at her mother's demise than she realised she had probably caused it: and that she would now have to spend more time in Chengdu organising funerals, friends and making announcements. And, worse, not seeing George for even longer.

The young doctor covered the deceased's face with her mother's coat and, as the shocked crowd melted away, he and Berenice exchanged details; he had already called an ambulance and it soon arrived, the medics checking her pulse to ensure that she was, indeed, clinically dead. They put her body on a stretcher and into the back of the ambulance as the doctor, whose name was Yu Xiaoning, offered to travel with Berenice to the hospital, which happened to be where he worked and to which she agreed.

Shocked but not sad, she sat in the back as the vehicle descended the mountain, her mother's body rolling slightly from side to side and bumping stiffly as the ambulance negotiated the winding route down into the city: although she felt she should chastise herself for her lack of feeling, she could not muster any emotion and rather found herself being more upset that she could not. Again, she wished that George could have been with her; but then, of course, he would have been an encumbrance in the current situation and another worry as she made all the inevitable arrangements. How lucky that Yu Xiaoning had been there. Good-looking – and charming, too. *It always took a tragedy to meet the nice people who mattered*, she thought. And with a chill of shame she wondered what might have passed if it had been him rather than Shuo, when none of this would have happened…

Chapter Seventeen

—⁂—

As soon as she was back in her mother's flat, she called George. He was hushed as she told him the news and – as expected – very sweet and understanding. They agreed that she could not leave Chengdu until all the arrangements had been fulfilled, but he promised to be with her for the funeral if he could. After a good, if alcohol-induced, sleep, he had actually wanted to tell Berenice the next time they spoke that not only did he have an estranged wife – a subject he always carefully avoided as much as Berenice had resisted asking – but also that he was finally going to leave her; yet now, this being the wrong moment, it would have to wait.

After the call, Berenice started working out all that she had to do. Now she was *completely* on her own; yet only just a day earlier, having organised her uncle's funeral, the chore was less onerous… except for getting in touch with her mother's friends. This would be difficult: her mother had not wanted to tell any of them about her brother-in-law's death and, after so long away, Berenice did not know who they were anymore or, indeed, if they were all still alive. She would have to look in her mother's drawers to see if there was an address book…

Also just as pressing was the fact that she had to tell work that she would probably be back much later than next Monday as originally planned – so decided to inform them now. She rang Mr. Chen's office but the call was answered by Natalya – who seemed strangely astonished it was her but had the tact – or was it a spited deceitfulness? – not to divulge that she had thought her to be no more.

"I'm afraid Mr. Chen's out of the office until next week," Natalya informed Berenice coldly.

"Well, would you tell HR as well, please – they'll sort it out in the meantime."

"Of course," Natalya agreed; but when they finished the call she did nothing. She had never liked Berenice. Or Shuo. Or the girl who would arrive on Monday to take Berenice's place. And appraising people of Berenice's return was none of her business, she thought – let them all sort it out themselves. And she smiled an evil smile at the chaos her inaction would cause to those three very good-looking people. Jealousy was one of her very many unattractive middle names.

After the call with Natalya, Berenice wondered whether she should ring Shuo to ensure the message got through – Natalya was notoriously and wilfully inefficient – but thought better of it: far too much had happened since they last met and that girl she had seen him with still grated within her. She would get back to work when she was ready. They would understand.

It would turn out to be a poor decision.

—m—

George, who had so looked forward to returning to Beijing and immersing himself in the beauties of Berenice, felt as if the rest of the week had had a pall cast over it; she, too, was now so involved with being the sole attendee at her uncle's funeral and then arranging her mother's that she wished she had never made the journey to Chengdu at all. She had, though, found herself weeping somewhat at her mother's death, which she had not expected; but the mother traditionally being the paramount and most respected family member in China had bestowed on her a feeling of contrition in her demise and she started trying to think of the good things about her rather than the bad. It was true that her mother had been wrong to allow what she had known about her uncle, but perhaps there were some mitigating circumstances after all; things were so different then and any support – whatever the situation – had been a necessary lifeline for her.

So, a feeling of guilt crept over her, not just because of her lack of understanding but also because, if she had not come to see her mother, then she would probably not have died. It was her fault: she had annoyed her mother – as her mother had done to her – but Berenice had unwittingly pushed her too far as a result of her short temper. She was her mother's daughter, after all – and perhaps she was not a little unlike her, which brought her up with a shudder. Although it might explain how she could suddenly dismiss Shuo so easily. She was a modern woman, she liked to think: but this guilt had made her realise she was still imbued with the traditions and history of her country.

Her self-absorption over, she found the criticisms of herself a wake-up call to whom she really was as a person and concluded – despite everything – that she wished she had been willing to forgive her mother earlier. Now it was all too late. Then she found herself thinking of George again, and what her mother had said about him: well, if she was correct and he *was* too old it would soon become apparent... and then she would be proved right. Just like she, Berenice, always wanted to be. Then the thought of the sumptuous weekend she could have had with George rushed in on her again and she found herself resenting it – then chastised herself again for being so selfish. Not knowing which emotion to follow, she just burst into tears and lay on her mother's bed, beating the pillows in frustration.

Sometime later, she woke up and started thinking of all she still had to do. Alone. She also wished she could have been back at work on Monday, fortified by George's presence and could therefore dismiss Shuo as an unnecessary embarrassment. Just as her mother had done to her...

As for Shuo and Lin Yang, they were looking forward to the next week for different reasons: she for the excitement of a new and stimulating job, he because he would be with a beautiful girl he could show off to the office without hiding the fact. It would be a great new beginning for both of them. Or so they thought.

Chapter Eighteen

—⚉—

It was Monday morning. After many weekend conversations with Berenice, where George had almost convinced her to allow him to come and see her in Chengdu, they had thought better of it: she would be distracted by him, the arrangements would be more complicated and ultimately they would see each other sooner in a convivial environment than if he had joined her. And her past life could finally be put behind her.

At nine o'clock, Lin Yang arrived at her new office; although she and Shuo had spent the weekend together, he had gone in a good half hour before her so tongues would not wag for somewhat longer. And he could make it look to the dreaded Natalya that there was nothing between them – until she found out, which she would. She knew of all the office relationships – official and not so – right down from the board, through the chairman and Mr. Chen's distractions to the canteen staff's various peccadilloes: nothing escaped her, which was why she was so despised and feared. Rumour had it that this was the only reason she was still there because too many people were in terror of her ever spilling a very large can of beans. She should have retired at sixty, of course; but her influence over – and knowledge of – those in higher echelons had enabled her to stay on, provided no-one ever discovered her true age. With all her garnered intelligence, though, that would never be forthcoming. It was literally a job for life.

Shuo's desk phone rang and a curt, waspish voice informed him that a Miss Lin Yang was in reception awaiting him. And please would he bring her up to her office with the form she had subjected her to fill in.

The lift took an age to come but, as ever, on seeing his lover in the foyer attracting appreciative looks and glances, the butterflies in his stomach became a swarm and he felt weak with joy – so much so that he stumbled as he held out his welcoming hand and fell headlong into her. Rescuing the situation, she took advantage of what had happened and embraced him, adding a kiss on the cheek for good measure so everyone would know that they were an item. Lin Yang had vowed there would be no silliness on that front – she was going to ensure that everyone knew about them. And that they would be a formidable and ambitious team.

They ascended in the lift and got off at Mr. Chen's floor, from whence they proceeded to his office. He was not there yet: characteristically, though, neither was Natalya. She had decided to snub them by going on her travels, Shuo surmised, gathering information as usual which would be useful to her; she had obviously decided to inconvenience this new relationship from the outset. So, knowing precisely why she was unavailable, they waited, so she could not accuse them of ignoring her when she returned. After fifteen minutes, Natalya did so, instantly annoyed that Shuo had read her motive. Switching her glance from Shuo to Lin Yang, she observed coldly: "Ah, you must be the new recruit. I hope you've brought the file I asked you to fill in."

"Indeed I have," Lin Yang replied, and gave them to her in a beautifully coloured folder.

Natalya gave this a peremptory look and tossed it onto her desk. "Well, I daresay Shuo here will look after you," she mumbled, and then looked up at Lin Yang with a dart-like look, adding, "He's good at that, I believe."

Shuo inwardly sighed and took Lin Yang's arm to guide her out of the tense atmosphere, but she was having none of it and was sweetly smiling, replying, "It's so good to meet you, *Miss* Beriskovska – I've heard a lot about you. I'll do all I can to make our relationship as harmonious as possible." She smiled sweetly once again as she shook her hand and then walked out, leaving Shuo somewhat stranded in her perfumed aftermath. As Shuo left, a slightly discomfited Natalya found herself thinking, *I'm going to have trouble with that one – she'll need cutting down to size.* Then the office was empty and she continued with her devious tactics alone.

Shuo took Lin Yang around the offices, introducing her to colleagues and pointing out the places she would need to know. One or two noticed that they seemed to be together as an item and resented it; others appeared to be glad for Shuo – but either way, it was what Lin Yang had planned: Shuo was hers and no-one else would influence him but her. He finally took her to their own office and introduced her to all its technology and idiosyncrasies, which she seemed to absorb without any difficulty; then she sat at the empty chair, switched on the computer and started to tailor it to her preferences.

It was instantly apparent to Shuo – and others who ventured into their office – that Lin Yang would be very good at her new job: she was instinctive, quick, made good decisions and addressed people with a business-like – if slightly offhand – nature. Like Berenice before her, she was able to turn on the charm where opportune and be clinical and cold where necessary. She could do that: she had the already-respected Shuo behind her.

—∞—

In Chengdu, Berenice was finalising her mother's funeral arrangements, which would happen on Wednesday. Having not seen her mother for many years until so recently, she had had difficulty knowing which contacts were still alive or had still been friends but, fortunately, had found a battered list of names and telephone numbers from her mother's mah-jong group, which eased the invitations and provided more details from one who had by all accounts been her mother's closest friend, Sun Hui Qing. Noticeably anguished at her friend's demise, Hui Qing nonetheless did all she could to help Berenice, who was extremely grateful – if only because it saved time and she would sooner find herself back with George.

The day of the funeral came, the service was conducted, and a meal laid on afterwards, which every invitee attended. Sun Hui Qing read some poetry and proclaimed all her mother's virtues – many of which had never been apparent to Berenice – and another friend said she would help Sun Hui

Qing to dispose of her mother's flat as, uncharacteristically in China, there was no other family extant – or, at least, known about.

After all this, Berenice found herself alone again for a day and decided to sleep in her mother's bed rather than the one she had been abused in. It was a final cleansing of the past.

Finally, on the Friday morning, she closed the flat door behind her, gave the keys to Hui Qing and departed Chengdu for good.

Her flight back to Beijing was uneventful, but she was sad that George could not meet her as he was recording a show at the time she was returning; he would join her later at her flat. She had declined the offer of going directly to his apartment: she had spent longer away than she had intended and wanted to be back in her space for a while to re-engage with her own life rather than so many others'. The weekend would be an orgy of happiness with George, which she would be better prepared for after a good night's sleep. When with George, that was not something she got much of…

—⟿—

After George had returned to a Beijing without Berenice, he had realised even more profoundly that he had never felt like this about anyone else in his life: he missed her intensely, was moody and depressed, could not sleep properly, and saw her in front of him wherever he was and with everyone he was talking to. She was omnipresent, like a guiding spirit: her laugh and smile intoxicated him, her body aroma drove him wild and her dress sense, fastidious attention to make-up and always wanting to look her best elated him. Unlike his wife: she had been pretty enough when they married some twenty years ago but had never had the fun, the clothes sense and the passion he had always imagined she would acquire over the years. She had also become frumpy and would seldom care much about what she looked like with friends, however much he pleaded with her. Like so many Western women, she had given up. Yes, Berenice was much younger than she, but he just knew Berenice would always do and look her best. And it was inspiring.

As a result, he had called Clarissa on the Sunday after his return to Beijing and continued in the same vein as the call he had had with her in Shanghai: that they should divorce as soon as possible. She could go off with Roger – which he had known about for ages but had been glad of, giving him a get-out excuse when needed – while he more discreetly went out with other women, mostly those of whom he met at work. And as he became more well-known and successful, so his ability to seduce them increased, commensurate with his fame and the size of his bank balance. In short, he had become a target for ambitious females – yet nothing had ever prepared him for Berenice. She was unique.

Knowing that Clarissa cared more about position and money than anything else, he had decided to offer her the house if she agreed to a quick divorce; it was a rambling old vicarage in rural Wiltshire upon which they had lavished huge amounts, and was worth over a million pounds, so she would not go short; and yet he just knew that she would fight and obstruct everything rather than just accept that their marriage was over. And Roger, a boring, effete little man who had become her lapdog, would benefit from his largesse – the only thing that really annoyed him about his proposed arrangement…

As expected, Clarissa had been belligerent, uncompromising and ill-tempered but, after an hour of wrangling and blunt, unpleasant accusations, she mercifully – but with a faux reluctance – agreed that it would be for the best. After haggling over the money and demanding one hundred thousand pounds as well as the house, she finally succumbed and said she would ring their solicitor the next day to set up proceedings. He had put down the phone in his apartment and exclaimed a loud, "Ye-es!" He would be free of her! Better still, he would soon be able to marry the love of his life, Berenice. Yes, she really *was* the love of his life; he just knew it. He could not wait to see her after her return from Chengdu the following Friday but for now, he would keep the divorce and its terms to himself: he wanted to see her reaction first-hand. After all, she had always been discreet enough never to ask whether he was married or not and he had kept away from the subject, too. She must have known; but that was the wonder of Berenice – she was, along with everything else, discreet.

How he loved her.

—⁂—

It was just before the end of another successful TV show recording that George's phone screen lit up to reveal a text from Berenice which stated, 'Arrived safely. Now on the way home. Very tired, See you tomorrow. Can't wait.' His spirits soared even higher and he went to the bar with the crew afterwards and ordered several bottles of champagne. He did not tell them what he was celebrating, but everyone could see he was very, *very* happy about something. Or, if they *had* known, two things. But he would tell no-one about either – yet.

The next day, he arrived at her flat at twelve noon and they immediately went to bed and drank the bottle of champagne he had brought, left over from the night before. They were both ecstatic at seeing each other and the love-making seemed even better than he remembered. After a snack and a much-needed shower, they decided to go to the Summer Palace which, to his shame, he had not been to. Berenice and he walked up the ancient walkways, appreciating the old and beautifully preserved wooden canopies stunningly painted with luminous colours depicting stories from China's rich history; Berenice had known some of these from her youth which – she shuddered to think – she had probably picked up from her dreaded uncle. But it did not matter: here she was, with the man she loved, showing him artefacts from her country's past which she was extremely proud of. And yet, she somehow had a feeling she would one day live far away from here. Probably in England.

That evening, George finally told her that he was married, but first that he was separated and he and his wife had – only a few days ago – agreed to a divorce, which was long overdue and not directly due to Berenice: she had merely been the catalyst. Berenice merely nodded and smiled; of course she had known he was married – how could such a lovely man not be?

"I wouldn't care whether you were married or not," she said simply after he finished telling her. George was delighted but, not wishing to overplay his hand, decided not to propose just then: it could wait a while as the news sank in and the divorce was over.

It made no difference to Berenice, though: deep inside, she knew that he wanted to ask her to marry him and would accept when he asked her but, like George, knew there was no rush. She could read his every emotion.

How she loved him.

Chapter Nineteen

—⁂—

It was Monday morning and as Berenice approached the doors of the office she felt a pang of reluctance to go in and stopped where she was. So much had happened since she suddenly left the building nearly three weeks ago: finishing with Shuo, meeting George, her uncle's and mother's deaths, the funerals… It seemed like a lifetime. And then there was the added complication of trying to avoid Shuo without raising any suspicions about their relationship – past or present. It was no-one else's business other than theirs.

She sighed; but just as she was summoning the courage to cover the remaining hundred yards between her and the door, she saw Shuo entering the building – hand in hand with the girl she had seen him entertaining that time before. What was *she* doing going into the office with him? She didn't work there now, did she? Or had the girl actually been with the company before but she had not seen her? A black cloud of insecurity descended upon her and she wondered if Natalya had passed on the message about her imminent return and her mother's death. She should have double-checked.

With a sudden determination to get to the bottom of this, she walked resolutely up to the revolving doors and entered the building. She would go straight up to Mr. Chen's office and make her presence known and, with a purposeful stride, went up to the automatic gates and swiped her card as usual, only to find she bumped into the barrier when the gates refused to open. Angrily, she tried again, to no avail. She then noticed that the security guard, whom she knew well, was watching her with a look of disbelief on his face, which concerned her; then he came over and swiped his pass to allow her in, saying, "Hi, Berenice, I thought…" But she had thanked him and passed on, not hearing the last part of his sentence in the general hubbub.

She took the lift and alighted on her boss's floor, then marched to the sanctum, where Natalya was piously sitting, the gremlin protecting Mr. Chen from all comers but whom she could see through the glass door of his office.

Natalya looked up as she entered and just said curtly, "Ah, I see you're back at last. Well, Mr. Chen's busy at the moment, but…" With that, Berenice saw Mr. Chen look up and see her as his face went white. Why? He quickly put down his papers, opened the door and beckoned her in, Natalya still protesting; all Berenice heard as the door closed behind her were the words, "…Sorry, I meant to tell you but…" and she was cut off.

"Berenice. It's so… lovely to see you, but…"

"But what?" Berenice enquired.

"Well, I… we… assumed you were dead."

This went like a bolt through her consciousness, so much so that she went weak and could only helplessly enquire, "Why?"

"The Chengdu plane crash. Someone said you had an aunt there... We thought you were on the flight – and as there was only one survivor and you weren't here, nor had we heard from you, we assumed..." He tailed off, not wishing to repeat those terminal words.

"So didn't you check?" she blurted out. "I mean, I told Natalya I was coming back."

"When?" he asked.

"The beginning of last week."

Mr. Chen looked past her at Natalya, who was standing next to her desk but facing him with a slightly triumphant, if concerned, look on her face.

"She never told me," he said quietly, looking down, then swore under his breath, the implication being that perhaps he could use it as an excuse to fire the woman at last. "Last week, you say?"

"Yes. I had some holiday to take. I left a message on your voicemail."

"But we thought you were on that plane – which crashed."

"Well, OK – but why didn't Natalya check with the airline? My name wasn't on the manifest, obviously."

"We tried. But the government suppressed all enquiries into the flight; I suspected there was someone on it who shouldn't have been, or whose death they wanted kept quiet, like a dignitary or something. They'd tell us nothing. But you could have told *me*."

"But I asked her" – as she thumbed in the direction of Natalya – "to tell you and HR. And, anyway, why would I think you thought I was on a flight I never went on?"

Exasperatedly, he nodded. "Indeed."

"As it happened, I did fly to Chengdu. But that was the week before last. I was intending to come back last Monday but my mother died while I was there so I had to arrange and then attend the funeral."

"Oh, I'm so sorry to hear that…"

"Well, at least we were together when she did so."

A silence descended upon the room. Then he said apologetically, "I'm afraid we now have a problem, though."

Berenice looked at Mr. Chen and waited for what this supposed problem was. "Erm… when you didn't come back and no-one knew where you were, I needed to find someone quickly to replace you. Quite honestly, there's no-one within the company who's anywhere as good as you are – and I couldn't ask Shuo: good as he is, his talents are better aligned in other ways. But he said he knew someone—"

"A girl?" she interrupted, smelling a rat.

"Yes. He'd met her and thought she might be a good replacement for you."

Met her? thought Berenice. *He's having sex with her.*

Mr. Chen was still explaining: "I was sceptical at first but after a week here it would seem she's very good—"

"Is she Shuo's girlfriend?"

Mr. Chen looked rattled at this question. "Erm, well… if she was, I didn't know it at the time he recommended her. I – we – obviously thought you were still together until, well, you know…" Berenice was annoyed people might presume this fact and that perhaps more had known about them than she either expected or wanted. "Now you ask, they do seem quite… well… close."

"So she's got my job, you mean?"

There was a long pause while he looked at her and then murmured, "Yes, I suppose you could say that."

"I see." Berenice was furious inside but knew she had to show a calm front. Mr. Chen was about to continue but she jumped in. "And what terms is she on? A trial? Permanent? A stop-gap?"

"Look, Berenice, this is all as much a shock to me as it is to you. But I'm a manager and I had to act fast. Under the circumstances, you can't blame me. But I like and respect you and won't let you down. Give me an hour or two and I'll come up with a solution. Perhaps I can promote you – it's well overdue, honestly, and I don't want to lose you. But there are people I have to talk to, as I'm sure you'll understand. In the meantime, please don't go down and have a go at Shuo – or Lin Yang. It's not their fault."

Lin Yang – so that was her name, the little minx. She'd show her; first, she steals her boyfriend and then her job. The fact that it had worked out wonderfully – having met George and discovered the most beautiful sexual experiences she could ever have imagined – was not the point. That little tart was going to get a piece of her mind. And even if the outcome *was* a better job, she would ignore Mr. Chen's request and use any new seniority to make Lin Yang's life hell. And Shuo's.

She smiled sweetly at Mr. Chen and just said, "Thank you, Mr. Chen; that would be wonderful. I'm very grateful. Shall I get back to you in a couple of hours?"

He nodded. Then, "No, I'll call you. I don't think I'll be long. Is your phone on, now?" It was her turn to nod. "Good. Then leave the building and go for a coffee outside or something. But don't go back to your office – it'll cause ructions. Off you go – I'll speak to you soon." He intimated for her to leave and she began to do so gracefully, only to have her departure arrested by his saying in a slightly admonishing tone, "I'm sorry if you've split with Shuo – you made a good couple. But I just wish you'd told me sooner of your situation yourself. It would have avoided all sorts of misunderstandings."

Berenice nodded. "Yes, I'm sorry."

She left his office, darting a filthy look at the implacable yet distinctly nervous Natalya on the way out. As she made her way to the lift, she looked back and saw Mr. Chen giving her a severe dressing-down. She smiled to herself: all in all, things were looking up all round.

The lift arrived but she did not leave the building: instead, she went straight to Shuo's office to embarrass him – and to confront his new little harlot.

—⁂—

In Mr. Chen's office, Natalya was being given a thorough tirade. Yet as she had been placed there by an influential government agent with links to the highest echelons of the government – and also the Kremlin in Moscow – firing her was a difficult thing for him to do: he could not risk falling foul of the city governor or it would be she who would stay and he would be out, cancelled, never to find work again. But Natalya had done this sort of thing before and he was her boss – much as she resented it. Well, she resented everything. So he toned down the rhetoric – actually more difficult than giving her the both barrels he wanted to – but made it clear in no uncertain terms that if she withheld information from him again as a result of her prejudices she would, indeed, be out. Even if it was he who suffered the consequences.

—⚏—

Her heart thumping, Berenice walked as nonchalantly as she could into her old office, but it was empty; she looked at her desk, which now sported the accoutrements of someone other than herself. There were pens, jotters, notes and highlighters all over the desk – not as tidy or organised as she was, she huffily concluded. Why had she been so stupid as not to ensure that Natalya had passed on the message? And she *should* have emailed Mr. Chen directly, castigating herself for being too proud to mention to Shuo that she was going away for a while and to tell their boss. Actually, she was unsure whether she should be angrier with herself than the others; but then, she'd never expected someone else would replace her so quickly – how could they? She was unique! Whatever the reason, her anger was suddenly worsened when she suddenly heard Shuo's voice outside; instinctively, she turned away from the door to face the window, so she could make the impact of him seeing her there, alive and well, all the greater. He entered and she spun round. But it was not Shuo: it was Lin Yang.

—⚏—

After Berenice had left Mr. Chen's office and he had then dressed down the recalcitrant Natalya, he picked up the phone and asked to speak to the chairman of the company. Unusually, he was available to talk and Mr. Chen explained the situation to him, with particular emphasis on the unsuitability of Natalya for the job she held there. Would there be any chance he could finally sack her? No, the chairman stated in emphatic tones. Reluctantly realising that there was no room for discussion, Mr. Chen proclaimed his request to promote Berenice and give her a more senior job. To this, the chairman was more compliant: if Berenice had been a fly on the wall at that moment she would have realised that her occasional flirtatious looks with the chairman had been worthwhile: he liked Berenice... So what sort of job had Mr. Chen in mind?

"Why don't we make her head of the department?" Mr. Chen enquired. "She has all the skills, she's personable, knows her way around the company, is great with design – and clients, of course... I think she'd be perfect."

There was a pause, then the chairman said: "So you'd demote the boy, erm... what's his name?"

"Shuo."

"That's the one."

"Ah... that could be awkward... he's very good – and he introduced Berenice to us, remember. And he works very well with the new girl, Lin Yang, too. I offered her a six-month trial contract, but so far she's doing very well and so I think I'll want to keep her. Shuo seems to be able to spot talent very well."

"What's *he* like at his job, though?"

"Er, extremely good." Mr. Chen was aware the conversation had changed angle and was slipping away from him: it appeared as if the boss was veering towards getting rid of Shuo as the price for giving Berenice an improved position.

"Hmmm. All right, then, do what you think is right. Just let me have the details when you've hammered them out. But if you really think the two girls will be better than the boy, then get rid of him." And the phone went dead.

Chapter Twenty

—⁓—

"Can I help you?" said Lin Yang as she entered her office to find an unknown woman there.

Having heard Shuo's voice, Berenice was momentarily disconcerted to see the girl in front of her. "Ah, erm, I'm... Berenice."

Lin Yang looked as surprised as she was. "Berenice? Shuo's ex?"

Berenice nodded, trying to hide the contempt she felt for this indignant intruder, even if it was partly her own fault.

"But I thought you were... Well. I thought... Shuo said—"

"That I was dead?"

Lin had come round to face Berenice at the front of the desk, so both their eyes were looking away from the door.

"Yes."

"Yes, that's true," said a shocked, tremulous male voice in the doorway. "In fact, *everyone* thought you were dead."

Shuo had entered the room and instantly read the situation. "Er, Yang… This is Berenice; Berenice, Lin Yang."

The two women looked at each other coldly for a moment, then Berenice turned to Shuo: "So why didn't you get in touch to tell me all that's happened?"

"I tried. You never replied. And, thinking of it, why couldn't *you* have told *me*?" This was said with a slight tetchiness in his voice. "We all thought you were dead. We – the company – had to move on."

"So what's your position here?" Berenice darted at Lin Yang.

"It's more or less your old position," Shuo replied for her. "But of course, she's not as experienced as you were – in this job, of course; in her previous job she was – so I now have more control over things than I did when you were here."

That's all going to change, thought Berenice. "Well," she said as she made for the door, "I hope you'll be very happy here in my old office with my old boyfriend," then turned dramatically to say, "but I doubt it," and swept out.

Lin Yang and Shuo stood open-mouthed as her presence and scent disappeared down the corridor. Shuo shrugged his shoulders and then, seeing a tear in Lin Yang's eye, rushed to embrace her. "It'll all work out," he comforted.

"Yes – but how?" said Yang, bursting into tears. In her mind, she was thinking not only of Berenice's barb but Shuo's comment regarding his superiority over her and her mental reaction to that was, *But I'm soon going to have as much control as you.*

As she descended in the lift, Berenice realised that she, too, had tears in her eyes. Whether it was out of anger, frustration, her stupidity or arrogance she was unsure. Perhaps it was all four.

—⁂—

Mr. Chen rang Berenice's mobile to find her in a small teashop not far from the office. He could immediately tell she was subdued, possibly upset; so was he. He had never intended the trade-off to be one for another and he wanted all three employees to stay. If only he could sack Natalya, who was the main source of all his problems... Yet he was, he had to admit, slightly angry with Berenice, too, as she and he had always had a good relationship: so why had she not got hold of him personally to ensure he knew she would be away for a while? He would have granted her any request immediately because she seldom took holiday; they both knew that Natalya was jealous, obstructive and manipulative so why did Berenice not be as fastidious as she usually was and ensure that he knew what she was doing?

"I've got a solution," he stated when she picked up.

"Oh?"

"Mm. I want you to be the head of the department."

There was a pause as Berenice took this in. "You mean, what *was* my department?"

"Yes."

"So... over Shuo and..." she couldn't bring herself to say her name, even though it was emblazoned on her mind, "... the new girl?"

"Effectively, yes."

"I see. Well, yes... thank you."

"Good. But there is a caveat. You must treat them all with respect. And don't make it too hard for Shuo – you wouldn't be here without his help – but I think the chairman wants to get rid of him in order to pay for you. But I won't have that, if I can help it, so I'll need your help."

"OK. Er, yes, of course."

"Good. And, Berenice, I really mean that: you'll have to use your charm on the chairman to ensure Shuo stays. Another thing – and this is strictly between you and me… Personally, I want to get rid of you-know-who as soon as possible – she's a malignant curse on our department. So, if I succeed, I'd like you to take over as my PA. But I don't know when – or if – that will ever be."

"Well… thank you. Again. I accept either plan." *That's the best route to becoming Mr. Chen's replacement*, she thought. Not yet, of course – and she owed him a lot. But in due course…

"Come back tomorrow – take the rest of the day off, Berenice. There are things I need to discuss. And smooth over."

Berenice consented gladly; how her life seemed to always turn out right. She must lead a charmed life, she thought… and she smiled and texted George. Life was good and now, with her mother's death and Shuo humbled, she was almost her own master. Yet she could not quite admit to herself that she was completely content. Her relationship with George was the only thing which seemed resolved and perfect, whereas with the other issues there were now new hurdles to surmount before she could survey all below her…

—⁂—

An hour or so later, after having smoothed things over with the chairman, Mr. Chen summoned Shuo and Lin Yang to his office and told them his plan. Shuo was quiet but understanding – he was that kind of person – but Lin was more resentful. She had just started doing this job, felt she was doing well and would prefer to report to Mr. Chen rather than this beautiful but determined girl she had only just met and who might challenge her dominance and progress over Shuo. She reluctantly but sweetly agreed, yet was now even more determined to make the most of the chance she had been given.

And, as a woman, she knew that this was what Berenice would be thinking, too. Poor Shuo: he would not know what had hit him…

Chapter Twenty-One

—◊◊◊—

Berenice told George her news and he was, as expected, ecstatic, although he admonished her slightly for not having organised her sudden departure very well. Berenice did not mind this observation from George but would have done so if it had been anyone else. Yet the fact that it had turned out so well trumped everything. He was having a quiet day and so they decided to meet up there and then and spend the rest of it together; her new job could start tomorrow. The weather was pleasant so they took George's car and drove as far out of Beijing as it took to find a patch of unspoiled countryside, a lengthy journey due to the size and number of newly industrialised areas of the city – thrown up with little regard for wildlife, aesthetics or ecology. But as the countryside became wilder and less developed, a calm descended on them both and the day was spent in harmony and mutual admiration.

—◊◊◊—

In the office, it was already a different story. Shuo was resentful that Berenice had effectively become senior to him and Lin Yang was showing signs of bossiness, tempered with the same resentment at what this stuck-up woman had done to Shuo – and to her, of course. But she intrinsically accepted there would be tensions, and also knew these would have to be subdued until after her trial period. Then, if the chairman and Mr. Chen wanted her to stay, she would go all out to remove Berenice.

Natalya, meanwhile, had left the office in a foul temper and was talking to the chairman; she felt she was being pushed out – and that was not in the agreed order of things. Her father and the chairman had been good friends and, despite the age difference of around twenty years, had supported each other for the benefit of communism and the absolute rule of the state. The chairman, though, was explaining to her that he was almost sixty and would be off in a few months to enjoy the rest of his life with his money and mistresses. And, to a lesser extent, his wife. So soon he would not be able to help Natalya – perhaps she should find a freelance position in another international company where – like their company – the rules could be bent more easily? This she did not want to hear: she wanted Mr. Chen's job. But now at least she could see the writing on the wall and that her deviousness and bile would have to be far more surgically applied than hitherto... With renewed vengeance in her blood, she thanked the chairman for his candour and returned to her office.

—⁂—

Mr. Chen had instructed some changes to Shuo's office so there would be more room for his new team, and this would be done in a day or two. Now he was waiting there for them; it was early and the turgid dullness outside the window was ignored in his feelings of optimism and exuberance for his new team. Whilst not knowing that there had already been a meeting of his three charges the day before – which he had expressly ordered Berenice not to do – he had wanted to be there to defuse any potential conflicts before they started. It was a wise decision, for while Shuo had accepted it and Lin Yang had put her feelings on hold for now, Berenice had decided to cement her ascendancy. George had instructed her not to show any animosities and to be gracious and understanding in her new, exalted position, especially as he had again chided her for the situation being largely her fault, despite mitigating circumstances. Yet, much as she loved George, she wanted to ensure that this past cycle of events remained beneficial to her; after all, she had been dealt a good hand despite her admittedly poor management of developments after the break-up with Shuo and she felt it incumbent upon her to regain her composure and innate perception of predominance.

Fortuitously, Berenice was the first to arrive, whereupon Mr. Chen started laying out what he wanted from her – and what he expected her to get from her team. There was, however, a barb in that he had decided overnight that Shuo should be the same level as she was, the reason being that he had been the conduit for both the girls' appointments and it would be unfair for him to be junior to either of the two women. As for Lin Yang, this would give her the impetus to strive harder. It was a good compromise, in his view, and would help things along. Yet it was not a view shared by Berenice. Before she could protest, however, the couple came in and further discussion on that particular issue could not continue. Mr. Chen availed them of his decision, which delighted Shuo but made Lin Yang suddenly feel like the junior partner who would have to do all the less glamorous jobs: this was not what she had signed up for. Yet while Lin Yang's diplomatic side overcame her internal annoyance, she vowed to get this pesky woman out of 'her' office through sheer hard work and ability. This sentiment – though not Yang's endgame – was precisely what Mr. Chen had envisaged: he had sensed there could be rivalry between the two girls and wanted to make this creative tension work for the company.

Mr. Chen's specific delegation of roles was that Lin Yang would do more to acquire new suppliers and designers – an area in which she had excelled in her first days at the company – and then help Berenice to enhance, deepen and fine tune these new relationships, suggest other avenues, promote design and fabric ideas and keep costs down; together, they would create innovative marketing to promote fashion trends which would build their company's profile globally. For his part, Shuo would be the dynamic instrumentalist who would take all these elements and create a department that would drive these things to happen.

Chen left the office with a spring in his step: he felt he had just created his best team and the chairman would be proud of him. In the office, however, the still waters he had envisaged would run deep...

—⁓—

The next morning, Berenice arrived to find that she had acquired a private cubicle for herself, next to – and connected by a glass door to – her old office, which Shuo and Lin Yang were now in. The atmosphere had the temperature of a freezer: Shuo was the only one making an effort to be civil, understanding and sympathetic but at one time had snapped at Lin Yang when Berenice was out for a few minutes as she was being so uncommunicative. Whilst it pained him to underline to Lin Yang the reality that she was on trial, still, he pleaded with her not to do anything to anger Berenice: it would only make things worse.

When the latter returned, the temperature warmed as Lin Yang tried smiling and appearing to help: the ploy had worked. Better still, Berenice had already begrudgingly accepted that Lin Yang possessed serious talent and indeed truly mastered her job: in the time she had been there she had developed a number of ideas, found some new designers and ingratiated herself with a number of exporters and local businesses. A slight glow of respect – however much resented – was beginning to be realised. And she had to admit that Shuo was a very good judge of whom to take on; not only herself, of course, but Lin Yang too. With an abrupt feeling of surprise, she suddenly imagined herself in bed with Shuo, having wild sex, all her patronising instincts swept aside in a wave of jealousy and desire; what was happening to her? Why had she never let herself go with him? Now Lin Yang had him: and she was beautiful – although not as refined as she was. Ah, yes – that was the difference: George was a man, not a boy: urbane, gentlemanly, intellectual, knowledgeable about how to caress her in bed… not just a quick, fumbling intercourse, which she was sure would have always been the case with Shuo.

Yet her growing jealousy made her feel that she wanted to find out.

—ⴵ—

That night, Shuo's sex with Lin Yang was exceptional again: she had noticed Berenice looking at Shuo in an unusual way and instinctively, as a woman, knew what it meant. She would not let it happen.

At the same moment, Berenice was putting George to the limits of his sexual prowess as if wishing to prove that he could keep up with how she now wondered Shuo might be – or even exceed that perception.

Both couples found themselves very tired the next morning.

Chapter Twenty-Two

—∿—

It was Friday and the week had gone well for the new team. The resentments and animosities were, for the moment at least, submerged, and Shuo had become more assertive, resourceful and creative. Lin Yang had spent more time out of the office chasing new contacts and, subsequently, had managed to avoid Berenice for much of the time. But past chemistry is a powerful equation and it was soon obvious that the tensions and aftermath of Berenice and Shuo's past would catch up. And when Lin Yang was out, there was time for the odd score to be revealed and debated.

In one such instance, Berenice had asked Shuo why he had so suddenly left her. His answer, "I couldn't bear to be with you but not ever make love with you," was readily understood by Berenice; what she could not understand was the speed at which he had found Lin Yang and started a deep relationship with her. When she asked him, he replied, "Because… I met her when you had exhausted my ability to live with you, for the reasons I've explained… and she was suddenly there, available and willing, and you weren't."

"So she was a substitute for me?"

"No – a release."

This shocked Berenice: she still hoped that Shuo would love her – at least a little – and that he would always have a light shining for her, even if she had no wish to reciprocate. But the brutality of his response was telling.

"So it was just sex?" she pursued.

"No. I loved you and wanted sex – I got sex with her and now I love her." That stumped Berenice and she went back to her work. But it unsettled her.

The following weeks entertained similar odd moments of exposition and each left the other slightly more intrigued. George and Lin Yang had been the catalysts they had needed to discover each other – but now it was too late.

Or was it?

It was almost inevitable that, one day, the two couples would meet. So it was that, on an early autumn Sunday afternoon at the end of September when the scraggy Beijing trees were tenuously holding on to their still slightly burnished golden lustre, the two couples had suddenly found themselves confronting each other in the grounds of the Temple of Heaven. As usual, hundreds of people were there, talking, walking and buying fripperies from the multitudes of traders, while other groups were doing tai chi, mellifluously waving to a hundred music players in the receding damp light. It was George who recognised Lin Yang as the girl in the shopping mall who had translated for him when buying the perfume for Berenice the first time he had visited her. They struck up a lively conversation while Berenice and Shuo looked on in annoyance. Shuo had forgotten the episode, of course, as most men do; but the situation was not lost on either him or Berenice. "I always remember a pretty face," had been George's parting accolade that particularly annoyed them, but Lin Yang was delighted – not just with the compliment but also that she could see it was discomfiting to both Berenice and Shuo.

In the office the next day, it was obvious that the encounter had made an impact on each side and that it had been the subject of much discussion the evening before between both couples. George was lucky in that he was the only one outside the office bubble – despite the fact that it was his carefree comment which had provoked such a spirit of resentment and mistrust. He was, of course, oblivious… but the event would have a lasting effect on the other three players.

Chapter Twenty-Three

—〰—

George's divorce was progressing well and his decree nisi was – according to his solicitor – pending; his wife was due to move from the family home within a couple of weeks and into a new one with Roger; the potential spoils of the house's sale had left George wanting to return to England – with Berenice – for a couple of weeks to find a house in which they could both live when not in China. He had formulated another game show for his Chinese network which was also stirring interest with both British and American channels, so the prospect of sumptuous houses in both China and his home country did not only appeal but would soon be financially possible.

Berenice had become somewhat subdued after the incident at the Temple of Heaven but as her reasons seemed trifling to him, he had dismissed them. Yet the mood was, more often than not, apparent; so to allay her concerns he finally decided to ask Berenice to marry him, and the trip to England would also be a perfect time to look for a mutually acceptable home there. Being an Englishman, he wanted to propose properly, and so organised a private room for the event in a very expensive Beijing restaurant bedecked with flowers, lanterns and history; it was situated in an ancient villa with Ming dynasty rooms connected to a corresponding series of corridors and courtyards. The evening came and they sat alone in the room, attentive waitresses beholden to any call just outside the door. After the meal and a delicious liqueur, he suddenly stood up, walked around to her side of the tiny table, dropped to one knee and took her hand.

"Darling Berenice—"

"Yes," she stated instantly and emphatically, with a concupiscent smile playing on her lips.

"Yes, what? I haven't asked you anything yet!"

"Yes," she said again, with a growing set of tears in her eyes.

"Ah… well, if you know the question—"

"Yes!"

"But I think I should just be allowed to ask it – just so I can be sure you mean it—"

"Yes, I do."

"But if there were any conditions you wanted me to make, explanations… don't you want to discuss them before you…?" He tailed off, adoring the look of sublime and tearful happiness on her face, while she shook her head.

She did not, for once, want to say the word, 'No', in case it was misconstrued.

"Well, then… Erm, darling Berenice: will you marry me?"

"Yes!" she proclaimed loudly, so much so that the two waitresses outside (who had suspected the reason for the occasion and had been keeping their ears ready for instructions) spontaneously burst through the door, smiling and clapping in the charming, discreet way that only Chinese girls know how.

This took George by surprise, but he grasped Berenice by the waist and kissed her passionately as the waitresses silently retired again.

It was another hour before two very happy people left the restaurant, inebriated by their high spirits and a celebratory surfeit of alcohol. The trip to England had been all but planned and it seemed that ecstatically happy times would lie ahead. And the night's passionate conjugation reflected this in its intensity and ardour.

—∾—

Deep inside, however, despite willingly acceding to George's proposal, Berenice's sudden wild imagining of missed sex with Shuo still troubled her. George had slain the demons caused by her uncle but, rather than be released by this, she occasionally felt she had missed an opportunity. She did not want to risk losing George and all that he promised, of course, but the thought disturbed her. When they were all together in the office she found herself looking at Shuo and Lin Yang and wondering what they did in bed together. Lin Yang obviously excited Shuo, but the feeling that she might have squandered an opportunity due to her frigidity constantly teased her. She loved George desperately, but he was quite a bit older than her; and although Shuo was still a boy in her eyes, he would, of course, grow into a man – especially if controlled by her! Yet the second she was in

George's company, her doubts evaporated like a puddle in a heatwave. She consoled herself that the trip to England would do wonders for all of them and looked forward to it with a renewed fervour.

On the eve of their departure, Berenice laid out what she wanted Shuo and Lin Yang to do while she was away; she was feeling optimistic and happy, and so found herself praising them both for their superb work to date. Both the chairman and Mr. Chen had noted how well the new trio were performing and all thought of dismissing Shuo had disappeared – although only Berenice had been privy to that possibility anyway.

It was mid-afternoon when Lin Yang suddenly proclaimed she felt unwell – a little sick and faint, accompanied by various minor pains she could not account for. Berenice immediately told her to leave the office and go to see a doctor, which Lin Yang gratefully assented to: she left soon after and notified Shuo she would see him back at his flat later on…

Once again, Berenice and Shuo were alone in the office: since the Temple of Heaven episode, Lin Yang had been careful not to leave them alone for too long if she could help it, not because she was paranoid but because she wanted to be privy to any discussions about work. Or their past relationship. Once she was gone, though, Berenice called Shuo into her adjoining office, her heart beating somewhat more strongly than she neither expected nor felt comfortable with.

"Shuo, I want to apologise."

"Er, what for?" Although he sensed what this might be leading to.

"For my behaviour in the past. To you, not letting you know about my movements, being so offhand… And, of course…" And she looked up at him.

"Saying 'no' all the time?" She had not expected this sharp reply from Shuo: in her mind, she had wanted, as usual, to control the conversation, but now Shuo had upstaged her. In fact, even she had not realised she was going to say what she had, or apologise, or anything like that; it had suddenly been an impulse she could not conquer.

There was a brief pause, which was awkward enough to need filling and, much to her surprise, she found herself saying, "It's Friday; as I'll be away now for a couple of weeks, let's you and I just leave the office and go for a drink."

Much as she was startled at saying this, it was nothing compared to Shuo's astonishment. "Er… yes; that would be nice," he stuttered, having had neither a moment nor the confidence to resist.

Berenice, of course, subconsciously knew exactly what she was doing – without really knowing why she was doing it; but now she was aware of being back in control of her life, she was loving it. So she continued: "We don't want Natalya or anyone talking, so I'll leave first in a few minutes when I've tidied up, then you can slip away a few minutes later. Why don't we meet in that ice-cream parlour we used to go to?"

Shuo nodded; there was a glint in Berenice's eye he had never seen before, and whilst it troubled him, it excited him, too.

Berenice just said, "Great," and got on with putting her office straight.

Shuo was weak and trembling as he put some files away and finished off emails to colleagues. Half-way through this,

Berenice breezed out with a cheery, "Bye," and disappeared. He put his head in his hands: there was still something irresistible about Berenice, and particularly so today; hence, he certainly did not want to cancel. Subsequently, after a few minutes, he shut down his computer, picked up his bag and left.

—⚹—

Lin Yang had finally managed to get to the front of the queue at the medical centre and was ushered in to the stressed-looking man behind the desk.

"What's wrong with you, then?" he asked without looking at her, as if a nobody in a line of somebodies. Lin Yang explained her symptoms and after he had asked the usual questions about headaches and any nausea, he asked her to lie on the couch while he examined her stomach area. For the first time, he looked at her directly and from then on seemed to register her attractiveness and the fact that she was a fellow human being, before asking abruptly, "Have you had sex recently?"

Lin Yang could not deny that she had – and lots of it, although she kept that to herself.

"Hmmm… Then I'd say you were pregnant."

This shocked Lin Yang to her core; she had been taking precautions ever since she had met Shuo… although the first night with him a few weeks ago she had been somewhat more cavalier as she had just wanted to snare him. Could it have happened then?

She asked that question, to which the doctor replied, "Well, it takes a few weeks for the body to start changing and that's when you start getting the symptoms you're having."

Lin Yang sat up and looked at her pretty toes and then on towards the floor, almost in the hope that it would swallow her up; she had no idea how Shuo would react and was worried he would dump her if he found out: they were both too young to have a child, either emotionally or from the point of view of maturity. They had even discussed that situation, almost as a joke, as something which could never happen. But now it looked as though it had, it was suddenly very daunting.

"Are you married?" the doctor asked with a slight sneer, as if to imply that he already knew the answer. She shook her head. "Well, you can get rid of it if you want." And he handed her a piece of paper which had been irreverently cut by blunt scissors and was obviously something he handed out a great deal. On it was an address and a website.

Perhaps I could just go and get it done without telling Shuo, she thought. And the sooner the better if she wanted to keep her new job – and keep that Berenice away from Shuo, too. She thanked the doctor and left, a somewhat more subdued and pensive character than the one who had entered the surgery an hour or so before.

And if she had known what was happening at that moment with her two work colleagues, she would have been even more so…

―❦―

Berenice and Shuo were sitting together in almost exactly the same place as a few short weeks ago. It was a very different

Berenice, though, in front of a somewhat uncertain Shuo. She had become more open, laughed more, was calm but animated – and looked ever more beautiful as a result. Shuo hardly got a word in as she told him of what had happened after she and he had broken up: how she had gone to his flat to apologise but he wasn't there and, of course, how she'd subsequently met George and how wonderful he was. Shuo also learned that her mother had died, but she had never mentioned it before – how strange was that?

Then she asked how he had met Lin Yang and he told her in no less detail – but neither of them mentioned the sex: that subject was taboo, personal.

They were both so relaxed and informal, and everything had been explained with such candour, that an hour went by without either of them realising it. Yet Shuo felt that behind the apparent openness, there was something Berenice was avoiding: she had told them all that she would be away for two weeks which, of course, Shuo knew: but he speculated that there was some internal barrier stopping her exposing the main reason why. For despite the reason given – that she was flying to London on Sunday with George to find a house in England for them to live in when not in China – Shuo was mystified: surely there must be another, more dominant reason for her carefree, ecstatic attitude? So the more he heard, the more he felt her choice of words were hiding something of far greater magnitude.

There was a lull in the conversation as each took stock of the revelations they had heard, when Berenice suddenly turned to Shuo and said, "This place is getting too busy; I've got a nice bottle of wine in my flat – why don't we go back for old times' sake and drink it?"

"What about George?" Shuo asked warily.

"Oh, I'm not seeing him tonight – he's recording one of his TV shows. I'll go over to him tomorrow to prepare for our trip to London on Sunday. Coming?" And without waiting for an answer, she stood up and started to leave, then turned to him and added, "Give me a few minutes' start... just in case," and walked purposefully out. Shuo waited, feeling like a little boy being told to do something by his mother which he could not – must not – resist; so he meekly waited five minutes, finished the melted remains of his ice-cream and left his chair to go.

What he did not know was that the subject she was avoiding was in addition to the one he suspected...

—⟋⟍—

Lin Yang left the surgery and found a small café in an old street where there were some smaller, more intimate shops that had not been razed to the ground in China's brutal charge for progress; she ordered a tea and sat, deflated, in a window seat, her thoughts swirling around her whilst fingering the already crumpled and damp piece of paper the doctor had given her. She decided to wait a few days to see if her symptoms re-appeared, in the forlorn hope that the doctor was wrong; but whatever happened, she would not tell Shuo yet, and if she wanted to have the termination she would do so without his knowledge at the best time for her. She decided to ring him and say that she was fine but was tired and would spend that night alone in her flat: it would give her time to think. That was the easy part... she could do what she wanted with him and get away with anything, he liked her so much. Then, like a shard of light penetrating the gloom, she realised at that moment how much she liked him too, and chastised herself for her occasionally patronising view of him. Nonetheless, she still desperately needed a night away from him to formulate a waterproof plan. Whatever happened over the next few days, though, she knew would be awkward…

She would not be wrong in that assessment.

—∞—

Shuo took Yang's call as he approached Berenice's flat, which only made him feel guiltier; he was glad she was fine but understood her wish to have a good night's sleep and that they would meet sometime tomorrow. He hung up and pondered whether to switch his phone off, just to avoid any embarrassment or misunderstanding should she ring again while he was in Berenice's company: yes, he should. He could restart it when he got home later. He did so, put it in his jacket pocket and rang the doorbell.

Berenice had only just arrived at her front door when she received a call from George. Aware that Shuo was not far behind her, she did not want to cause any problems with her intended but also knew she could not dismiss his call quickly – it was so unlike her to do that with him. So she tried to speed things up by saying she had just got home and was desperate to reach the bathroom: fortunately, he was about to record a show and had to be quick himself – but not quite quick enough for him to hear Berenice's doorbell ring as he rang off.

Berenice pressed the button to let Shuo in and quickly put her phone off, then unplugged the landline in the hall; she kicked off her shoes, sprayed a little perfume onto her neck, re-did her lipstick, added a colourful silk scarf to her already immaculate appearance and opened her front door as she waited for Shuo to appear. He was just about to knock as she did so, and the bunch of flowers he had bought on the way almost ended up hitting her in the face as he leant forward to do so. They both laughed and Shuo realised again how much more relaxed she was than when he had been with her. *Well, that's what true love does to you*, he thought.

Which was why he was completely astonished by what happened next.

Chapter Twenty-Four

—⟋⟍—

Having heard Berenice's doorbell ring, George had been momentarily surprised at who might be ringing his fiancée's doorbell in the early evening but was soon embroiled back in his new show. It was a pilot, so he was even more pernickety than usual and was currently involved in a dispute with the director about the opening wide-shot which would set the tone for the whole series.

He was uncharacteristically bad-tempered, too, as his soon to be ex-wife had also been causing disruption, as ever wanting more money and a greater share of the spoils from the divorce, which was now holding up the decree nisi. But George felt he had jettisoned enough in her favour and the proceedings had subsequently reached a stalemate, made more difficult by the time difference between England and China: it also gave her solicitor more time to prevaricate as this excuse could always be used to drag things out further.

Soon, though, the dispute with the director resolved, (George got his own way as usual by asking him face to face if he really *did* want to direct the whole series), the show was underway and going well: at times like these, fripperies such as demanding ex-wives and doorbells were swept away in a grand orgy of harmless fun.

—␒—

Berenice closed the door behind Shuo, took the flowers and put them in a vase on the table, intimating that he should follow her into the small sitting-room. Shuo instantly noticed a solo picture of George on the sideboard and another one of he and Berenice together; there were also tell-tale additions to the array of pots, ornaments and trinkets which would seldom have been bought by Berenice but would have been gifted to her by an admirer. Disconsolately, Shuo realised he was in a different league to George and that he had been mad to ever think he had a long-term chance with Berenice. He sat down as she went to the kitchen to get the wine out of the fridge and came back with this and two glasses, along with some delicious snacks he had neither seen nor tasted before. To his surprise, Berenice did not sit on the small chair opposite him, which was her usual perch, but next to him on the sofa. She poured the wine and handed him his glass, waving at the snacks as if ordering him to take what he wanted, which he duly did.

"So, here we are again," she said after a few moments of observing him. "And so much has changed since you were last here."

Shuo felt he was being tested somehow: he wasn't sure how or why but there was a sense of wicked vengeance as a faint smile played around her lips. "Yes," he admitted, "and who thought that the next time we'd meet alone socially you'd be engaged?" He observed her reaction to this: he was aware once again how so much was different about her now – not just because of being away from office restrictions but also how she looked at him; her gestures, too, seemed more receptive than they had ever been when they were together.

"Well, I'm not engaged tonight…" She smiled at him.

Shuo coughed, a tiny piece of the crispy snack having got stuck in his throat – so much so that he went red and coughed all the more violently until he took a slug of wine to wash it down. Throughout all this, Berenice just observed him, hardly moving. He was on his own. "Sorry, went down the wrong way."

"That's all right…" and she leaned forward to fill his wine glass. Shuo felt he was being teased, played with, especially when she continued with, "And I'm not married yet. So, it's time for me to apologise properly."

"Hmm. You said. But I'm still not sure why, really." She just stared at him, the smile getting slightly wider, so much so that Shuo felt he had to say something – which was just what Berenice had wanted. "Well, it was frustrating, yes; I loved you very much and found you extremely attractive… but you would never let yourself go."

"Things have changed," she said starkly.

"Of course. You've met the man you love and…"

"And?"

"Well, I suppose I have, too – Lin Yang, I mean!" He laughed awkwardly.

"She's nice."

"Yes… And George seems nice, too, I have to say. Bit old for you, but…"

"He's a man," she replied simply.

"Ah, I see. So you think I'm still a boy?"

She did not answer, which made Shuo certain that she felt this was, indeed, the case.

"But younger men have their attractions," she continued. "I just needed a *man*" – she emphasised the word – "to make me realise that."

"Right." He squirmed a little: this was an awkward conversation. And the tiny bit of snack food was still niggling his throat.

"I now realise what I was missing with you," she suddenly blurted out. "And I want to make it up to you, for all the hurt I caused you."

"Ah. Er, could I have a glass of water?"

"Have some more wine. There's another bottle if we finish that one."

Shuo did not know what to do – she was playing him so cleverly, but he still could not comprehend where this was all leading to. He got up to get some water himself, only realising as he did so that his penis was stiff enough for her to observe its excited state. So he sat down again. She picked up his glass and held it in front of Shuo's mouth. He took it and gulped it down, dislodging the annoying particle in his throat. "That's better," he admitted.

Berenice moved slightly closer to him and he observed that a button on her blouse had been undone, revealing a hint of black lace brassiere underneath. His pulse rate was now reaching fever pitch and his manhood was beginning to hurt due to the restriction of his underwear.

He looked at her. "What do you want?" he asked uneasily.

"Isn't it obvious?" she replied cheekily, staring into his eyes. "I said I wanted to make it up to you..." And she brushed his forelock, her beautifully manicured hand with its painted nails sending a shiver of pleasure across his face and down his neck and spine...

"Are you trying to seduce me?" he croaked hopefully but in disbelief.

She said nothing but moved her lips to his and gave him a light kiss, then withdrew slightly and looked at him.

"But what about George? You're engaged."

"And so are you to Lin Yang – in a way. Well, you soon will be."

"What do you mean?"

"You'll soon find out." She had been fairly certain that Lin Yang had left to see the doctor because she was in the first throes of pregnancy but would not elaborate, just in case she was wrong. Shuo seemed none the wiser. What he *had* become wise to, though, was that Berenice was suddenly rubbing the now very large bulge in his trousers.

"Come on," she said. "We may not get another chance... And no-one will know – neither Lin Yang nor George." And with that, she stood up and took off her blouse, then her brassiere; her small, pert breasts were glistening with desire and erectness. Shuo was astonished – she had never let him see them in full before; only some irresolute fumbling had been allowed before the shutters had always come down. She was magnificent to look at. As he was clueless how to react to this complete *volte-face*, he just sat there and watched as she then slowly, sexily and seductively removed her stockings and then her minimal panties until she was totally naked. A small dewdrop of white liquid appeared at the entrance to her vulva, and she looked sheepishly at Shuo and said, "I'll wait for you in the bedroom," then walked away with the occasional backward glance in his direction. After a moment, when he had checked that he really was *not* dreaming, he stood up, took off his trousers and pants, then his shirt and shoes, and made his way towards the bedroom, noticing as he passed the hallway mirror that his erection was bigger than it had ever been…

—٭—

After the successful recording of his show, George rang Berenice but was disappointed to get only her voicemail. He left a message but then rang her flat, only to find that the number was unavailable. He wondered whether he should go to her to check if she was all right but resisted the temptation as Berenice would accuse him of being paranoid; she had probably just taken a sleeping-pill and gone to bed early. He would try again in the morning. Being tired himself, he went home to bed and slept soundly.

As for Lin Yang, she had been annoyed that Shuo had not rung her to find out how she was feeling but – as she did not know what to say to him under the circumstances – decided not to phone him either and would plead tiredness and falling asleep early when they got in touch next morning…

—٭—

In Berenice's flat, the two participants were experiencing different sexual experiences to what they were used to: for

Shuo, it was the realisation of a dream which he thought had forever eluded him, and while Berenice was not quite as passionate as Lin Yang in the finer arts of relentless love-making, he found he could gently cajole her into the more extreme acts he had learned with Lin Yang – but wished so much that he could have been able to re-interpret them with Berenice many more times; she was emollient, understanding and willing without being ravenous, as Lin Yang always was: as a result, he could take longer to reach climax each time and this, in its own way, was more fulfilling. As for Berenice, because Shuo was able to sustain himself for longer and delay, this sent her into guilty paroxysms of orgasmic pleasure – even if it was all a bit rough and desperate… In this, she was glad to be with George, as she would surely be unable to keep up with Shuo and his youthful exuberance for too long. Indeed: for after one particularly prolonged session, when she had climaxed several times in succession before he allowed himself to release, she just said, "It was unforgettable," before falling back, exhausted.

And so it would be. Unforgettable. For both of them…

She knew she should not have engineered it; but deep inside she was so glad she had. And so was Shuo. It meant that they had finally closed the relationship on a mutually satisfying note. And how: more importantly, Berenice had achieved what she always wanted: total dominance. And she had one over on Lin Yang, too.

Chapter Twenty-Five

—〰—

The next morning, Lin Yang was woken by her phone ringing; she had suffered a sleepless night but then drifted off in the small hours and was annoyed that she was being woken at what seemed to her such an early time. A look at her clock, however, made her upset for another reason: it was just gone eleven o'clock and, knowing it was Shuo's ringtone, was piqued by the fact he had not rung earlier! For his part, Shuo had just arrived home; he and Berenice had woken together late, too, and suddenly Berenice had worried that George might be concerned about her and come round, only to find her in flagrante delicto with Shuo and the end of everything. So Shuo had been somewhat bundled out of her flat as soon as the hour had been realised. While Shuo had dressed, she reconnected her landline and switched her phone back on – to find three messages from George enquiring if she was well – two of them that morning. She had rung him back immediately from the bathroom, after telling Shuo to be as quiet as possible, only to find that George was only a few minutes away. She said she had overslept and could he delay his arrival for a while, especially as they had agreed not to meet until tomorrow; but no – he was nearly there and wanted to see the love of his life as soon as possible, which meant that she had to rush into Shuo while still talking to George, signalling and imploring him to make his exit as swiftly and quietly as possible. She then gave him a quick kiss as she raced back into the bathroom to finish cleaning up: Shuo, still dazed and astonished by the events of the previous night, was reluctant to leave and was not a little annoyed at being ejected in such a hurry.

George was still asking Berenice why he could not get hold of her either at home or on the mobile and she made the excuse that there must have been an internet problem which her mobile phone was reliant upon: as for the landline, she had purposely unplugged it as she had received a couple of unpleasant calls. George sounded wary of all this, as well he might; yet he took it in good heart and rang off just as Shuo was silently but reluctantly closing the door behind him.

With Shuo gone, Berenice then ran into the bedroom and ripped off the sheets and pillowcases, tossing them into the washing-machine and starting it off; she then scoured the flat for any sign of Shuo's stay and noticed – to her horror – that he had left his watch behind by the bed. She whisked it away and put it in her bag so she could discreetly return it to him at work on Monday. Oh, no! She was off to London with George tomorrow! She rang him immediately to tell him, but Shuo had just left the lift and was about to depart the building – whereupon he saw George parking his car. He relayed this fact to Berenice and told her to hide the watch, at the same time realising he could not exit the flat without risking being seen by George. Berenice agreed and rang off as Shuo quickly went up a flight of stairs to hide on the next floor. As he turned the corner out of sight, he heard George entering the building – he even had his own key! Breathless and now fully awake, Shuo waited until George had entered the lift and then quickly left the flats in as discreetly a fast way as he could…

Berenice had just finished showering – the fastest of her life – and rushed out to greet George in the hallway wrapped in a towel and still dripping with water. She had done her best to ensure that there was no relic of Shuo's illicit presence still visible and asked George to make himself a coffee as she finished drying off and getting dressed.

"Why bother?" he asked her cheekily, but she being exhausted and not a little sore, implied to him that her curse was starting and it would be best to put off any sex until it was either over or she was sure it was a false alarm. He pouted with an aggrieved acceptance and she escaped into the bedroom, still drying off as she went; she had put Shuo's watch at the bottom of a drawer by the end of the bed, covered by clothes, and then saw that there was one of his long, straight black hairs on her bedside table: that was one thing that could never be explained away! Her hair was not Chinese black – it was permed and dyed a slightly dark russet colour: George's hair, although straight, was a mousey brown flecked with grey… She picked up the strand and tried opening the window to dispose of it, only to find that the casement was jammed shut: so she put it in her palm and went back to the bathroom to flush it away, only to find George there, washing his hands. So she apologised and ran into the kitchen to put it in the bin: panic over! She could not do this ever again, she stipulated to herself: it was too deceptive and open to discovery...

A few minutes later, George was finishing his coffee in the sitting room, perched on the very sofa that Shuo had only vacated a few hours before. She went to kiss her fiancé as she apologised for not being ready for him and was soon kissing him as if nothing had happened.

But she knew it had – and was glad of it.

—◊◊—

After having left the flat in such a hurry, Shuo knew he had to go and get another watch before he saw Lin Yang as it had been an early present from her; also, Berenice would not be back for over a fortnight. Fortunately, he and Yang had bought it together and so he knew exactly where to go and, after his escape, had gone to buy another identical one for himself so she would never know. Which was why he had rung her so late. And also why he, too, stipulated to himself that he would never do anything like that ever again. But, like Berenice, he was glad they had. It was now closed. And on the most beautiful note possible.

Best of all, they were friends again...

—◊◊—

Berenice was trying to pack her suitcase for the journey to London with George the next day before going back to his flat with him. Being tired and unsure what to take to a country she had never visited before, she sought George's advice. He offered to take a look at what she had in her wardrobe at the moment she had just left for the bathroom. Suddenly remembering that Shuo's watch was there but unable to leave at that precise moment, she arrived back in her bedroom to see George looking at that very watch, a few clothing suggestions already placed on the bed.

"That's a nice watch," he commented, putting it back under the clothes in the drawer. "I've seen one like that before, but I can't remember where..." and closed the drawer to look in the one below. "I wonder what a man's wristwatch is doing in your clothes drawer, though," he said mischievously, casting her a knowing look. "Ex-lover?"

Berenice reddened and was grateful he had looked away from her as she tried to supposedly, nonchalantly, turn to leave the room to recover, only casting a cheekily dismissive aside to him as she left: "Something like that, yes." She was glad she had never told George about her uncle and her subsequent antipathy to sex until she had met him, so he would not have drawn any conclusions from that... Now, though, she could never tell him! She went into the sitting-room and put her face in her hands, her heart beating wildly. "A long time ago," she added.

"Really?" he called back. "Looks quite new to me."

She said nothing to that, pretending not to hear, but sat for a moment and breathed deeply.

Her heart rate was just returning to somewhere near normal when she heard George call her again, saying, "Berenice? What's this?"

She froze – had Shuo left something else behind? She hardly dared to return to the bedroom but – whatever it was – she knew she had to confront it head-on…

—⚬—

Lin Yang had welcomed Shuo back with a passion which he was too tired to reciprocate in his normal athletic way. Perhaps it was the vibes she was giving off? Had he surmised her secret? She had all but decided to tell him her news after all – but not yet. Not until she had had the chance to try a pregnancy detecting kit. So the day passed peacefully, even if Shuo's tiredness surprised her – he was normally so lively. And virile…

After a few hours, they decided to go for a walk and, when they passed a pharmacy, she decided to go in and 'get a few girly things she needed'. She suggested Shuo went for a coffee on the other side of the street while she did so and he readily agreed: he did not enjoy shopping with Lin Yang – she took so long!

A few minutes later, carrying a bag which she alluded to as being 'mostly make-up', she joined him for a drink and then they sauntered around some more shops before returning to her flat. Once there, she closeted herself in the bathroom and applied the test. She had to wait for twenty minutes, which seemed like an eternity and which had Shuo coming to the door to see if she was all right; then she looked at the result.

It was true: she was pregnant.

—⚬—

Berenice entered her bedroom and saw George looking at something in his hand, which was too small for her to see. Her concerns rising, he suddenly pulled it open with his hands to reveal the tiniest see-through green and black lace panties and bra set he had ever seen. Her heart was relieved, though – she had bought them a few days ago as a tease for George when they got to London!

"Oh, you weren't supposed to see those," she exclaimed, laughing out of relief as much as embarrassment. "They were a surprise!"

"Want to road-test them now?" he replied with a grin.

"No! Naughty boy! Wait until we get to England!" And she left the room in relief, hoping that there would be no more panics that day: she had had enough of them already.

That evening, Berenice was very glad to leave her flat for the safety of George's, where no more nasty surprises might present themselves; she was so happy to be alone with him again and so adored his company… Yet her secret excited and empowered her because, discreetly, she knew she had an advantage over him he did not know about…

Chapter Twenty-Six

—◦—

Back in the office the following Monday, Lin Yang eventually told Shuo about her pregnancy. She had wanted to know for sure that Berenice really had left the country and would not suddenly appear at the wrong moment; also, she chose their office location because she didn't want Shuo to storm off if he was unhappy with the news: he had to stay in the office for work.

His reaction was muted; worried, certainly. Perhaps not surprised but also astonished that this should happen to him when it was his first serious sexual relationship; because it had never happened during his time with Berenice – whatever the frustrations – on that score he had always been safe.

His unexpected wild night with Berenice had also, inevitably, confused the situation: his emotions were stretched – torn, even – and all the things he had desired with her before he met Lin Yang had suddenly come to fruition – but not in the way he had expected: this had left him adrift like Odysseus on his tiny ship, being drawn one way or the other by competing sirens, each ensuring certain death.

So he took the news quietly and left the room for a few minutes: his emotions were too jumbled to think straight and he needed a few minutes' reflection; Lin Yang was sympathetic and glad, at least, that he did not seem angry, just confused. It even crossed her mind that, his being such a boy, he had not realised the possible consequences of his virility... but then brushed that aside as ridiculous. Her contemplation was not helped by seeing the hawkish face of Natalya watching her from outside the office – who then moved swiftly on when she had become observed.

After a few minutes, Shuo returned; his demeanour seemed brighter but he was still quiet. "What would *you* like to do?" he enquired.

"You're the man" – she nearly said 'boy' – "and I'd like to know what your decision would be."

"I think... well, I—"

"I can get rid of it, if you want."

The abruptness of her comment shocked him; it was cold and emotionless, as if there was no compassion or thought for him in that abrupt statement. Yes, he had thought that this might be the best option but, being a sensitive male, had tried to see it from Lin Yang's perspective and had reckoned she would want to keep the child. And also – possibly – get married. Her apparently curt dismissal of both those possibilities troubled him; and after the very recent happenings with Berenice, he still held out the prospect of a candle for her, however remote and faint that hope might be.

"Hmm..." was all he could say. Then: "So you don't want to get married and have the child?"

Now it was Lin Yang's turn to be confused. As a woman, of course she wanted the child… one day. Just perhaps not now. Or with Shuo – at least until she had known him better for longer. And she had latterly started wondering whether she might now become more successful than he – especially if she could engineer the removal of Berenice. Without that calculating presence in the company, she would be better able to control Shuo, who still seemed to be under Berenice's aegis rather too much.

If only she had known. But then, being a woman, she possibly did…

—๛—

Berenice had never flown first-class and the experience was an eye-opener. George had negotiated prime flights in his contract with the Beijing TV company and stipulated two seats each time if necessary – when he thought his wife might accompany him. But she had shown little interest in ever coming to China and George had speculated she cherished the time away from him and could so spend intimate hours with Roger. How glad was George of that now! From being disgruntled and annoyed, he was now supremely happy and his prescience when negotiating that contract now meant he had the love of his life sitting next to him for nine hours. Not only that, but they would be plied with good food, champagne and enjoy a comfortable bed apiece.

Berenice was also blissfully happy… yet she still found herself thinking about Shuo too much: that irresponsible but wonderful night had not killed a ghost as she had subconsciously intended but fermented other emotions. Shuo's innate naivety was obviously a counterpoint to George's urbanity and smoothly knowledgeable common sense, but she was aware that she could always be the superior partner with Shuo – whereas, with George, she was at worst subservient and at best his equal. Yet as the plane flew on, she told herself firmly that her life was now with the latter; he adored and pampered her and she wouldn't have had the chance to have a home in England as well without him. One feeling she could not suppress, however, was the fact that she had got one back on Lin Yang – whether the girl would ever know it or not.

—⁂—

Shuo had found himself in a deep depression after the conversation with Lin Yang. He had lost the love of his life, found another, tasted the forbidden fruits of the former without expectation, then found he could be a father – but the girl whom he had impregnated was dismissive about keeping the child and spending her life with him. Yet he did not know if that was what he now wanted and rapidly came to the conclusion that he had been used by both women. Loving each of them, though, meant he could not make a decision: he was at the behest of one or both of them. If he married Lin Yang, then he would be the junior partner as she became aggressively dominant; but he knew Berenice would stick with George or – if that man became incapable of fulfilling her intense dreams – he might be an occasional guest in her company which would mean being unfaithful to Lin Yang. It was a difficult situation for him and he was powerless to influence things either way. Except by forgetting Berenice or leaving Lin Yang.

Understandably, neither of those options were attractive to him.

The next day in the office continued to be difficult; he knew Lin Yang was torn between keeping the child or not, but was aware that he did not seem to have an opinion she would listen to either way. From a work perspective, though, she seemed turbocharged without the restrictions of Berenice and was pushing for changes and new contacts as if in a race to cement them as *faits accomplis* before her return. Shuo realised he had effectively become a bystander – yet he was supposed to be running the office… He began to wonder, then, if he should leave and find another job, so allowing the two women in his life to battle it out between them. He might be able to garner the spoils later on, he mused, yet it was not a solution that attracted him.

Lin Yang came into the office and put her notes on the desk, then slumped into her chair. She looked away from the desk to the window, avoiding Shuo's concerned look as a tear ran down her face.

Tentatively, Shuo enquired, "What's the matter, sweetheart?"

"I'm tired," she snapped, then burst into tears.

He went and put an arm around her shoulder, wondering whether his affection would be spurned; but she sat there dispassionately, the tears silently rolling down her cheeks.

Then she turned to Shuo and said, "I can't do this job *and* have the baby, and I don't want to go away for maternity leave, so I'll have to get rid of it."

Shuo looked at her and turned her face to his so she had to look at him, then said quietly, "Darling Lin Yang, if that's what you want, I'm with you. We can have a baby another time, if you want. You're… – we're – still young. And, yes, we have to make our progress in this business while we're this age… So, I'll help you to do whatever you want."

"Oh, thank you," she blurted, and threw her arms around him, kissing him again and again. "I knew you'd understand."

"You arrange it and I'll pay for it."

She stopped crying and looked at him. "Oh, I'm so happy with Berenice not here. She's such a poison in this office; I feel she's watching me all the time to see if I slip up. And you still seem besotted by her. Tell me you don't love her anymore."

Shuo had wondered if this would ever be a question Lin Yang would throw at him, ever since Berenice had returned; now she was asking it and – as he was as confused now as Lin Yang – he found himself hesitating, which was not what Lin Yang had wanted.

"So you *do* still love her," she said, got up and went to the window. "I thought so."

"It's more complicated than that," he found himself saying. "We had a relationship, it ended, then I thought she was dead, fell in love with you and then she came back. Please try and understand my feelings as I have just understood yours. It didn't work out with her, I got you in here at the company and she returned. Of course there are going to be imbalances. But I do love you." She looked at him. "And one day, I want our child," he added. "But just not now, if that's what you want, too."

She looked at him. "You've had sex with her, I just know it."

Shuo stared at her. "No… no, I haven't," he stuttered. "We never had sex – that was one of the problems—"

"I don't believe you. I think you've seen her since she came back. Women know these things…"

"Well, you'll just have to believe me. There's nothing I can do to prove I haven't. And I don't think you should ask her when she returns," he added hopefully. "It wouldn't be a good career move."

Lin Yang looked at him. "OK," she said eventually. "But I'll be watching you. Both of you. In the meantime, I'm going to sort this out."

He opened his arms and she mercifully accepted the gesture, throwing her arms around his waist, too. Then they kissed again and he added again that he loved her, which she reciprocated.

They went back to their desks. As he did, Shuo noticed Natalya disappearing down the corridor. She had probably witnessed the entire episode.

Chapter Twenty-Seven

—◊—

"Which of those two girls are you actually going out with?" Natalya darted at Shuo a day or two later when he had gone up to see Mr. Chen in his office.

"I'm not answering that, Natalya; it's my life and therefore none of your business."

"Mr. Chen might think so," she observed sardonically.

"Then I'm sure he'll talk to me about it," Shuo responded as he went in. Needless to say, Mr. Chen did not. All he wanted to say was how well he thought things were working out with him and the two girls, and to discuss some operational improvements. And company profits were up, helped again by Shuo's little department. "Lin Yang is a success," he added. "You have a good nose for talent."

There was the usual visible permafrost on Natalya's face as he left the office. Shuo just smiled.

—◊—

In London, Berenice and George had gone to his flat, which was situated near the centre of the city in Battersea. Berenice instantly liked it there: the old buildings, spruced up for a gentrified clientele, restaurants, artisan shops and a market... and leafy roads leading to two commons where people played tennis, jogged and walked numerous dogs. It was so different to the brutalism of Beijing, even if the newer tower blocks in her home city were now of a reasonable design, whereas her perception of London generally was that buildings were thrown up when a space occurred without much thought for the surrounding aesthetic. The flat was a ground-floor conversion in a house of moderate size which was typical of its era – a bow-fronted late Victorian terrace home with a tiny front space and small garden at the back, of which she soon realised there were millions. It was comfortably furnished and very clean – so much so that she felt he must have a cleaner, but he said no, that was not the case; it was very English and she felt much at home there, even if many of the ornaments and photographs harked back to previous girlfriends and events. And his wife – which George swiftly swept away.

On that score, there was a mountain of mail on the doormat when they had entered, much of it needing intense perusal and signatures for the pending divorce. This made Berenice feel good: he was doing this for her – well, primarily, she cautioned herself. After the long flight, they took a shower and went for a walk across the common; the light was fading a little and the chill winds of late autumn were rustling the trees and causing minor storms of falling leaves. George put his arm around her shoulder and she placed hers around his waist. They seemed so right for each other and the air was so much fresher than Beijing that it seemed easier to breathe. It was all part of the sense of being in England, which she had read so much about. And now, here she was and – on first impressions – loving it.

What made it even more interesting was that he took her to a pub which stood overlooking the common – an English pub! She loved the atmosphere, the people laughing and drinking, flirting, eating, and generally being at one with life. And the appreciative looks she received as they entered made her feel good, too, after an initial few moments of apprehension. A number of George's acquaintances there came over to say hello and he introduced Berenice to them as his fiancée from Beijing, which caused some surprise as none of them had known he was divorcing Clarissa. She also noticed a degree of envy: she was going to enjoy being in England!

—⁓—

In Beijing, Lin Yang had just come from making an appointment to have her pregnancy terminated and would see a specialist the next day to ensure it was not too late for the procedure. It was easier without Berenice in the office – in fact, everything worked better without her superior demeanour lording it over all of them – and even Shuo seemed happier and more relaxed. Indeed, they were getting on so well that – even if he *had* had some recent dalliance with Berenice – she was willing to overlook it provided that the woman never came back. But that was the problem: she would. So she hoped that Berenice would marry George and stay in England forever; then she could control Shuo and build her importance in the organisation until she was running the whole department – or even the company! Getting rid of this embarrassing pregnancy was the first step – yet its happening had focussed her mind: she had become more objective. If it worked out with Shuo then a happy and fulfilled life with him was a distinct possibility.

So she upped her determination that Berenice would have to go.

—⁂—

After a couple of days in his London flat, George told Berenice that he had been contacting estate agents in Wiltshire to find a house they could live in when not in China. With the divorce from Clarissa supposedly almost upon him, he suggested it would be a good idea to go and see the house he had shared with her as she had just vacated it for her life of intended Elysium with Roger; but he felt that there were too many ghosts there to expect Berenice to want to live in it. He craved a clean start with Berenice, too, and did not desire any distractions from that. As soon as the nisi came through, he would marry Berenice in order to get her visa application started: any dual nationality problems could probably now be surmounted as he had made good contacts with elite Chinese officials and his ability to make money for their economy through globally successful TV shows would stand him in good stead. And if the British authorities were less forthcoming, they could live most of their time in China and he would return to England only as necessary.

The next day they drove into the countryside: he had shown Berenice the sights of London and now she was yearning to see the unique scenery she had heard so much about. It was not a disappointment: once off the M3 and A303, the green beauty of the undulating fields and woods of Wiltshire, punctuated by the pretty villages, local stone and cheerful people – that last point in stark contrast to London, she admitted to herself – made her feel happy, relaxed and even more in love with George than ever. It seemed as if she had the whole package and shuddered when she thought it might all be taken away by some unforeseen circumstance, such as his finding out about her wild night with Shuo…

They eventually arrived at a large, beautiful, stone-built Georgian building in its own grounds virtually in the middle of nowhere: even before leaving the car she knew she had fallen in love with it, whatever the past partner of her intended may have done to it. On entering, she almost intuitively found herself mentally re-arranging and re-decorating the interior: after all, this was what – in a different environment – she had been doing at her job in Beijing. Although that was fashion, she could apply her knowledge and ability with design, fabrics and colour to furnishings, ornaments and materials; she just knew she would be good at it.

George had entered the house and become strangely subdued: seeing his home of many years denuded by Clarissa of many of its objects and daily devices cast a sombre spell on him and it took Berenice a while to get him out of it.

"Darling," she said, "we can make this place wonderful again. Together. What's missing is only a bit of 'us', and once that's been applied you'll see the house in a new light. Trust me."

He threw his arms around her, and a warm, wet presence on her cheek made her realise he was crying. "Thank you, darling," he eventually replied. "You're so wonderful… Yes, it would be better to stay here if you're not put off by it. And no moving bills or extra taxes, either. But we're staying in a hotel nearby so you'll have the whole of tomorrow to change your mind if you *do* decide you don't want to live here. After all, we'll be looking at some other properties around here tomorrow, so it's your call if you find you'd prefer somewhere else."

But she did not want somewhere else. She just knew she wanted to live *here*. Desperately. Beijing suddenly seemed such a long way away – and how lucky was she to have the opportunity to live in either of two great cities *and* the English countryside to boot? She had been blessed. Even if it was all indirectly due to Shuo…

—∞—

The procedure had gone well: Lin Yang had had the termination on the Friday to give her the weekend to recover, and Shuo stayed with her and pampered her, administering to her every need and whim. This made her realise again that he was the sweet, caring man she had always thought him to be and that her escalation into a prominent position within such a prestigious company was all to do with this lovely person. And yet the looming return of Berenice hung over her and dampened her spirits. So much so that, on the Sunday afternoon before her re-appearance, Shuo took in a cup of tea to her but found her in tears.

"What's the matter, darling?" he enquired.

She looked at him intently then said, "That woman is coming back tomorrow!"

"Ah. Yes… Well, that doesn't matter. We're fine now that…" And he motioned towards her abdomen. "I think it was causing you concern about the speed of things… us, the office. Now we've got a perspective, we can be together without worry."

Lin Yang looked at him again, her doe-like brown eyes like dark pools of desire which could drown a ship, let alone Shuo's soul. "I think we should get married," she said starkly; then, before Shuo could reply, continued, "and then if this – "and she waved at her pelvic area – "happens again we can have the child. But not for a few years until I'm running the office – without… *her*." That last word was said more harshly than the rest of the sentence, and Shuo noticed it – but he said nothing for a moment as she looked at him. Then, he said simply: "Do you really love me that much?" Lin Yang found herself nodding, tears rolling down her face. *Emotion. That's how to get what you want*, she was thinking. Yet she also found that she did actually *believe* she loved him and that, perhaps, she really did mean what she had just said. How a pregnancy – even a terminated one – affected one's passions!

"I'll ask you to marry me when you've conquered these emotions," Shuo stated simply.

She was astonished: he had intuitively understood the feelings inside her, which made her love him more – he was so attuned to women's sensibilities: how many men were there like that in the world? Not many: yet here she was with one and she vowed she would keep him, whatever. "I think I love you," she said.

"I *know* I love you," he replied – as the face of Berenice flashed across his mind.

That was it: Berenice was going, Lin Yang determined – and the sooner the better. Whatever it took.

Chapter Twenty-Eight

—ᘜ—

The divorce had at last been finalised and it was promised the decree nisi would come through soon. George and Berenice, having decided they would like to retain his house in Wiltshire, had had frantic last-minute negotiations with Clarissa and her financially ravenous solicitor and offered her a good deal more than the asking price in the settlement to keep it: indeed, as soon as this had been agreed, they had started re-arranging things to fit Berenice's ideas of interior design into it. A number of shopping trips to Southampton and Oxford Street in London had given her a vast palette of ideas, designs and colours to draw on, and she had enthused and astonished George with her creativity and ability. He knew the house looked 'tired', which reflected his years with a wife whom he probably should never have married; yet, as so often in life, it is often the bad things which eventually influence good outcomes, so he revelled in Berenice's plans. In short, he anticipated that the house would become a showpiece – and all thanks to her.

Their two-week break had gone, it seemed, in the space of four or five days, and soon they were back on the plane and heading back to Beijing. As the aircraft started its descent through the viscous, leaden pollution of her home city, she found herself wishing she was back in the fresh green fields of Wiltshire or the buzz of London and wondered whether, in time, she would be able to make the break completely. Her thoughts and any guilt relevant to Shuo had dissipated and she just looked at it as a process which had had to be resolved.

Yet it would not all be plain sailing: life is not like that.

—ɯ—

Shuo and Lin Yang had determined to be in the office when Berenice arrived back and had arrived very early to ensure it; but Berenice had still beaten them to it. Yet, instantly, they noticed she was a changed person: there was none of the usual sullen objectivity or perceived threat of being upstaged that had been her trademark before; instead, she was bright, happy and engaging. She had brought them both small gifts from London, too; also, they could not help but see a subtly ostentatious diamond engagement ring but resisted asking about it for fear of Berenice retorting that it was none of their business – a response which had often been truculently administered in the past. Yet within minutes, she had proclaimed her news – but had altruistically waited until Lin Yang had left the office on an errand in order to tell Shuo privately first. She called him into her tiny office.

"Dear Shuo," she began, but he had instinctively understood what she was about to say and interrupted her with, "I know – I can see. I'm very pleased for you. Congratulations." Yet his delivery was joyless, sad.

Looking askance to ensure Lin Yang was not returning, she said, "Shuo, you're still very important to me and a wonderful friend. What happened a couple of weeks ago was a realisation of that. It was also a realisation that the door is closed on that side of our relationship, however liberating it was. And I don't regret it for a moment. In fact, it was a cathartic moment in my life."

"And mine," replied Shuo flatly. "But I suppose I had hoped… deep down—"

"Shuo, you have Lin Yang now. She's better suited to you than I was. And younger." She was about to say 'and more beautiful, too' but thought better of it – and also had no intention of gilding the lily, so continued, "And now I have George and you must understand that, without your actions, I would never have met him. So I have that to thank you for, too."

He nodded. "And, dear Berenice, I wish you well, too," he added melancholically, and slowly left the office just as Lin Yang returned. Berenice felt sorry for him in one way but relieved and vindicated in another. It had all gone according to her plan. Just as she liked it.

—ɷ—

Since Berenice's return, Lin Yang had changed her opinion about her boss but still wanted her gone: after all, how could she progress whilst that talented and inspirational woman was still there? Yet happiness in love was obviously a powerful concoction, she concluded, and, like a whiff of perfume, it was rubbing off on her, too; indeed, she and Shuo were now settling into a balanced and mutually reliant couple as well. The petty jealousies which had arisen when Berenice had first unexpectedly returned all those weeks ago had now virtually vanished, despite Yang's continued underlying wish that Berenice were somewhere else.

Life's convolutions, though, have a habit of delivering unforeseen results and benefits – as the protagonists had already experienced – and so it was that Lin Yang's wish would suddenly, unexpectedly, become fulfilled…

Two weeks later, Berenice announced that George had been instrumental in landing her a job within the set design department at the television company he was working for and so she would soon be leaving. Shuo was crestfallen, as if she had died once again, but things had moved on so much with Lin Yang that he soon got over it; after all, his former temptation would now be gone and their friendship had blossomed in a different way. Now he and Lin Yang, too, had an open run at happiness together. And he and Berenice could always meet up from time to time – either privately or all together as a group. As for Lin Yang, she was delighted, too, yet it was tempered with an unexpected sadness: she recognised – and was honest enough to admit – that Berenice had taught her a tremendous amount and, despite her different talents, without Berenice's influence she might not have succeeded as well as she had.

The day of Berenice's departure was marked by a small leaving party in Mr. Chen's office, who was visibly depressed at Berenice's leaving – less so, Natalya. All the main clients that Berenice had introduced to the company were there, too, and, of course, Shuo and Lin Yang. Mr. Chen had even invited George to attend: he was intrigued to meet this mystical Englishman who had whisked his prize employee off her feet and would take her to a foreign country. He was upset, however, to find that George was only a few years younger than he was, but in much better condition! Natalya was just annoyed. As always.

Chapter Twenty-Nine

—⁓—

As winter became more intense, and the winds from the Mongolian steppes became bleaker, colder and more intrusive, Shuo decided to offset the impending meteorological changes by asking Lin Yang to marry him. But her answer reflected the approaching season rather than the last days of summer, which was not what he had expected. She told him she was not sure and could he give her some more time? For, now that Berenice had gone as she had wanted, Lin Yang could be more of a free agent: having had the constrictions of Berenice's presence removed, it allowed her to be the titular head of the office she so craved. For practical reasons, Shuo had been happy to stay in the outside office: but Lin Yang had had designs on moving into Berenice's for many weeks prior to her actual departure. Shuo, being the gracious person he was, had been happy to oblige – not realising that it would give Lin Yang a superiority complex which he had not anticipated.

As for Berenice, her new job in television design had started well; the more confident and outgoing nature fostered by George was making her popular in her department and she was soon promised more scope to design the sets and moods that they were intended to convey; and when, less than a fortnight after her arrival, a drama producer asked her to design some quintessentially English sets as she 'knew' about England, she did so with aplomb – but not without a certain amount of help from George!

Life for them was good; their relationship was strengthening and their marriage in Beijing had been announced. The last vestiges of George's marriage to Clarissa had been swept away and Berenice had boldly ordered online some new fabrics and colour schemes for their home in England, as well as some new furniture, which they could pick up on their next trip there. All of which found George's approval. In Beijing, her flat was going to be renovated: they would live in George's flat – which was in a better district than hers, closer to the studios and newer – and keep hers for a rainy day if George lost his pre-eminence or she needed a bolthole. Her inner soul told her this latter course was the pragmatic one, especially as they could now afford to keep it empty.

—៣៣—

The changed office dynamics since Berenice's departure had increasingly created further doubts and contradictions in Lin Yang's mind. Although she was technically in charge now, she knew that she owed much of her elevation to Shuo, as well as her new responsibilities and a certain foundation for her life. Yet despite appreciating this, she felt there was something missing in him, even if she could not exactly put her finger on what that was. And it did not help that she often wondered if Berenice had thought this, too. She spent so much time trying to resolve the reasons why she had perhaps loved Shuo less when Berenice was there that it was clouding her ambition – all of which was continuously underlined by her concerns that something had once gone on between them. In fact, it had started to obsess her, then soon became a source of depression. She liked conclusions, not delusions. She had been a girl when she met Shuo and quickly became a woman, whereas she felt – increasingly – that Shuo was still the boy she had met by the pond. She therefore wondered if this was what Berenice had also concluded – but would have been angered if she had said it and would have defended him! In short, her emotions were becoming severely unbalanced...

A couple of weekends later, when she had gone for a walk on her own whilst Shuo played basketball, she was sitting in a small café and suddenly found herself being talked to by a man from Sweden. At first, she was annoyed by his presence and mild persistence, but something about him stopped her from walking away and soon she was in deep conversation with him, her basic English and his inadequate Mandarin causing wild laughter as they tried to converse. But the main thing she realised was his apparent worldliness; he knew things she had never heard about, let alone discussed – even with regard to China! Suddenly, the penny dropped: he was older, more intellectual and better dressed than her boyfriend: a man – and that was the key. Like Berenice with George, there was something a mature, wiser man could offer – wiser because Europeans had not been closeted within a country stifled for decades by political dogma. And as she spoke to him, she surmised this lack of knowledge was stifling her, too – she needed to foster a more enquiring mind. She should start reading more: books, literature, newspapers… and this admission, along with the easy confidence of this stranger opposite, set her pulses racing…

—⁓—

She felt nauseous: not about anyone or anything – just nauseous. She had returned home late from the studios and was relishing a lie-in the next morning: George was in England for a few days negotiating terms for another TV show and also instructing builders and decorators over some changes Berenice and he wanted instigating in their English home. Her first set had been built and had worked well, despite the whims of a tyrannical director who – like so many – had had no clue what he really wanted. So she was not feeling unwell for any spiritual reason: it must be something else. With a shudder, she wondered whether she was pregnant. Then, she wondered why she shuddered – or was it a thrill of happiness? Life was good, past concerns had evaporated, she had a super new job… was this the icing on the cake? Their wedding was still awaiting a firm date as the divorce decree nisi still had not come through but, when it did, they had decided to organise a celebratory party a little time later in England after their marriage in China: so what was frightening her? She had no mother or father to tick her off for being 'naughty' before marriage – and her uncle was dead, too: not that he would have had anything to teach her about propriety!

No, it was the sudden realisation that she might become a mother. She knew George would be delighted – he had not had children with his first wife and always regretted it: now she could fulfil him even more than she knew she was doing already. And with that thought, she felt indescribably happy – elated, even – as if any weight on her mind had disappeared into thin air. She lay back and rang George – it was late afternoon in England – and soon heard his warm, comforting tones, which seemed so close even when over five thousand miles away.

"Darling, I have some news for you…"

"I hope it's good news…"

"Well, I think so – I feel as if I'm going to have a baby!"

"Oh, that's marvellous! Oh, my goodness. Oh, I'm so happy…!"

"Well, I mean, I don't know *definitely* yet, but I just feel as if that's the case…"

"Never mind – find out soon! Oh, I can't wait to see you to kiss and embrace you."

This ecstatic response went on in much the same vein for a couple of minutes before he had, reluctantly, to go. Berenice put the phone down and sighed with pleasure, a contented smile on her face. Then her countenance darkened as a thought struck her: what if the child was Shuo's?

Chapter Thirty

—◊—

His name was Berndt and he inhabited Stockholm. Despite trying repeatedly to resist him, she had found herself unable to leave the café; attracted to his easy charm and ability to defuse embarrassing misunderstandings with witty jokes – which she seemed to understand despite her paucity of English – she was just drawn to him. It seemed intuitive. When she had tried to leave, he pushed a business card into her hand and charmingly but offhandedly told her to get in touch if she wanted to – no pressure. But it would be nice to see her again – preferably before the weekend, when he would be flying back to Sweden. She was torn; but she finally managed to walk away and forbade herself to look back, the hubbub of noisy people serving as a distraction to her febrile emotions. He followed her out of the door into the busy street. No, do not look back – if she turned around, it would show she was interested… but if she didn't, she might regret it forever. So she decided to glance back and, if he did the same to her, then she would contact him. If not, then that was that...

—∭—

Such was the unease in Berenice's mind that she wondered whether she should have the child terminated; she wanted it to look both Chinese and Western, as a way of proclaiming an East-West fusion. So the possibility of the child being only Chinese-looking sowed considerable concern. She was annoyed with herself for not having thought of that possibility before ringing to tell George the good news – or should it have been Shuo? No, she could never tell him: that would open a whole new can of worms.

She spent the rest of the day in a subdued state of mind. If the baby was born and it appeared to be the product of her and George, all would be well... But if not... how would she explain that away? Although she had been with George for six months now, the night with Shuo was only seven weeks ago: no, that didn't bear thinking about. It *had* to be George's – she had made love with him several times since then. Yet she hurriedly did some internet research and discovered she could get a DNA pregnancy test to determine the father. The downside, though, was that she would have to get a swab test from either Shuo or George: how on Earth could she manage that? Well, George was away and she did not want to waste time, so it had to be Shuo, somehow. Well, she would have to come clean and tell him. She thought of how she had told Lin Yang to go and get a pregnancy test and now she was doing it herself – for somewhat different reasons – and would therefore could get a paternity test device at the same time.

She shuddered again – this time because if it *was* Shuo's child, not George's, then she was in a bit of trouble...

–∾–

Lin Yang looked back. Just as Berndt did. She reddened and smiled, quickly turning away – but enough to show that she had connected. He was lovely. She would get in touch.

She went to where Shuo was playing basketball to find him waiting for her. "Where have you been?" he asked curtly. "I've been here for ages."

"Oh, sorry – I went for a tea and lost track of the time."

Shuo was obviously annoyed and, as they walked home, she wondered whether Berndt would get annoyed by something so trivial. In fact, as the evening progressed, she found herself wondering about his reactions to just about everything. She did love Shuo, of course: but... Perhaps she was lacking some excitement in her life? She was with Shuo both at home and in the office, but she did not want to leave her job: with a feeling of guilt, she wondered whether she wished Shuo would leave to work for another company, which would hopefully have the effect of their looking forward to seeing each other in the evenings and at weekends again. And then she could take over the office more easily. It was a tempting thought. As was seeing Berndt again.

–∾–

In the office next morning, Shuo was surprised to get a call from Berenice. Lin Yang was, fortuitously, out of the office: that was the first thing Berenice asked.

"Yes, she is," he answered warily.

"Don't react to what I'm about to tell you, just listen." The old, peremptory Berenice. She continued: "When we had that evening together…" Shuo wondered what was coming next, hoping she would ask if they could meet again.

"…we did something we had never done before."

Shuo waited.

"There can, obviously, be consequences to what we did."

What was she up to? Normally, she was so direct.

"Ye-es…"

"There's a faint chance I might be carrying your child." The blood drained from Shuo's face and seemed to pass straight to his nether regions, where the possibility of having a relationship – or at least, a familial connection – with Berenice again made him wildly aroused.

"I see," he said, with a slight catch in his voice. "So, what do you want to do about it?"

"Well, as you know, George and I are marrying soon… and I stupidly told him I was pregnant before I realised the child could also be yours."

Berenice has made a mistake? She's becoming human after all, he quipped to himself!

She continued, "So I need to know whether it's your child or his. Could you bear to do a paternity test for me?"

This astonished Shuo: in one sentence she had admitted a mistake and also asked him a favour; that had never happened before. Normally, she would have just told him what was what and that would have been it. She must be in love. Sadly, not with him but with that older man.

"Er, if it means I can see you again, then yes."

There was a pause, then: "Only for the purpose of getting a swab test from you."

Ah, back to the normal Berenice... "OK," he acquiesced. "When?"

"As soon as possible, please."

"I could pop out in an hour or so for a 'meeting'," he suggested.

"Great. I'll come to near you. Let's meet in the ice-cream parlour we used to go to. Is Lin Yang in the office all day today?"

"I'll look in her diary." He went into the little office which had belonged to the love he was now speaking to and looked at Yang's computer, just as she returned to the office.

"What are you doing?" she asked, a little vindictively.

"Just seeing if you have any appointments today," he replied casually. "Someone needs to know when you're around."

Lin Yang just nodded as they passed each other and Shuo went back to his chair as Berenice asked, "She's come back?"

"Yes, that's fine," he stated officiously.

"Great. About 2:30?"

"Excellent." And he put the phone down.

"Who was that?" asked Lin Yang.

"No-one special; you'll be in the office for the rest of the day now so they'll probably pop down soon."

"Oh." And she started to make a phone call. It was unlike Shuo to be so unspecific and it niggled her. What was he hiding?

Actually, she didn't mind too much: these days, she was somewhat insouciant about Shuo's occasional lack of clarity and knew that whoever wanted to see her would call again if she was not there. Shuo left the office, and she noticed he looked both concerned and happy at the same time. Strange boy! She put an appointment in her calendar for four o'clock: *See Jong Lau for a colour match test, Tien Lan Fabrics.* It was a new person from a new firm she was going to see.

Actually, neither existed at all. She had just had a nice call with Berndt and was going to see him.

Chapter Thirty-One

—⚭—

Berenice had already arrived at the ice-cream parlour by the time Shuo did, and he could not help thinking that she looked a little guilty, as well as even more beautiful than ever before. Pregnancy often did that to women, he knew, giving them a radiance that was almost surreal, and this was certainly true of Berenice.

However, whilst friendly, her demeanour was brusque and she obviously did not want to waste too much time chatting. She came straight to the point: "Shuo, thanks for coming at such short notice and for helping me. In my bag is a swab: would you mind taking it into the gents' and swabbing your saliva from inside your mouth for me? Then just put it back in the container, screw the top on and give it back to me."

Shuo thought for a moment. "You know I'd do anything for you, Berenice...But..." She looked slightly askance at this but was about to give the test to him when he added, "But that evening was so wonderful that if you *are* pregnant by me, I want to be able to see you – and the child – from time to time. It's only fair."

Berenice had not expected any conditions and it stalled her for a moment. Then she retorted, "I don't think that would be a good idea."

Shuo looked pleadingly at her. Then, he took the proffered swab and said, "All right," and walked away while she ordered his favourite ice-cream for him on his return.

Shuo went into the cubicle and looked at the slender phial she had given him. He was upset that she had been so dispassionate: he understood that she had to protect herself from any hint of impropriety with him on that fateful night but still wished there was more understanding of *his* feelings than she had shown. A wave of anger swept over him, fuelled by a sense of betrayed emotion, but he loved her still so much he could not bear to think the child could be his – for her sake, rather than his – as it would cause her so many problems. How could he best help her, this beautiful, forceful but inscrutable woman? The problem, though, was that whatever the right or wrong decision might be, he would still do anything she asked of him…

As he pondered the dilemma, someone came into the toilet area, coughing: he heard the man spit into the basin, then say, "Oh, God…" A thought crossed his mind: it was someone who was speaking English… He waited in the cubicle as the man finished his business and then peeked out to take a look at him: yes, he was Caucasian – probably American. The man did not bother to wash his hands and left, still coughing slightly, and the door banged behind him. Shuo looked in the basin and saw what he had failed to rinse away: could he really do this? What if the man had a disease which Berenice could then ascribe to Shuo? Well, that was a risk he had to take: the man was Western – that was the point – and had looked healthy enough the few moments he had observed him, despite the cough! And if it helped the love of his life then it would be worth it: she would believe her child was George's. He dipped the swab into the sputum, twisted it and put it into the phial, turned the top on tightly and went back to Berenice.

—ᴍ—

When he got back to the office, Shuo found that Lin Yang had gone out and, through curiosity, looked at her calendar. At four p.m. was the entry: *See Jong Lau for a colour match test, Tien Lan Fabrics.* No address. That appointment was not there before… He had not heard of that firm, either – good: Lin Yang was doing what she did best, which was to meet and develop new contacts.

He got on with his work but could not help thinking about Berenice and what he had done for her. If the man was found to have an illness then he could easily explain that away. Yet, if the child *was* his, it would be obvious – at least after a few years – by which time he would be well out of her life. But that saddened him greatly. It was his secret, though, and no-one else ever needed to know it.

—ᴍ—

Lin Yang had met Berndt and, after some awkward first moments, had found herself in amusing yet deep conversation with him again. He was perhaps a little older than she had thought, despite his trying to look younger in clothes that were more casual than the ones he had been wearing before. They were of a good quality, however, and his light brown, thick hair, complemented by a moustache which she had not particularly noticed the first time she had met him, gave him a military air. *That will have to go*, she mused, *if I start a relationship with him.* A relationship? What was she thinking? A few days ago she had admitted to herself that she was very much in love with Shuo! What was going on here? Well, she had been troubled by the termination procedure and it had made her emotional. Yes, that was it. And now those very same emotions were telling her that she found Berndt's airy personality and lithe physique very attractive... Yet she did not want anything to 'happen' before his departure the next day: that would be far too soon, so just play along for now. Then see whether he ever came back to Beijing. That would be the crunch point, perhaps. But not before, please...

Wanting the results as soon as possible, Berenice had sent the paternity test swab off immediately, along with the necessary blood sample she had taken herself. If the two DNA samples matched, it was Shuo's child: if not, it was George's. George would not be back for another few days and if the baby was Shuo's she might just have time to terminate it: she would tell George she had had a fall or something, and lost it. Never mind, they could try again, could they not?

The evening was drawing in and the blunt chill of winter was in the air, helped by a slight breeze which had blown the worst of the pollution away. Being fresher than usual, she decided to go for a walk to calm her nerves. She had received many plaudits for her set design at the TV studios and everyone seemed to like her, so as she had taken an hour off to see Shuo, she decided not to go back there and make up for it tomorrow. That was one of the things she really liked about her new job in television – it was so much more flexible than working in a regimented office. People came and went, but as long as the job was done, deadlines were met and meetings were honoured, all was well.

As she wandered around, she vaguely peered into the cafés and shops that were illuminating their lights in the approaching darkness, their spaces filling up with the young of Beijing. The city was becoming more garish by the day, and it was reflected in the clothing of those attending; when she had started work only a few years ago there had still been an unofficial dress sense: dour. Now anything went.

She was just about to return to the warmth of her flat when she saw a face she knew. She took a step back and looked again: yes, it was indeed whom she thought it was. Expecting to see Shuo as well, she was then surprised that the person the girl was with was not him at all but a Westerner who was not only pleasantly dressed but somewhat older than Shuo. And it looked very much as if they were *not* discussing business. Was Lin Yang having an affair? For Shuo's sake, she hoped not; yet the body language was certainly not that of a business meeting, and when he leaned across the table and kissed her, Lin Yang did not withdraw but lingered. She *was* having an affair! But Berenice could not tell Shuo. No: he had been so kind and understanding to her that it would be a horrible thing to do. And if she had told him, who knows how he would react? He could be quite emotional and, as a thwarted man on two occasions, he might – wittingly or unwittingly – let out their secret to George. She walked off with a quick step and went home, even more troubled than she had been when she left it.

—ɱ—

An anxious Shuo was waiting in his flat when Lin Yang finally caught up with him; but it was not in person, as they had arranged: no, she rang him to say that she was not feeling well and would go back to her own flat that night, not his. She had apparently bumped into an old friend after her appointment at the fabrics company and had had a drink or two too many: she was very sorry, but she would see him in the office the next day. Yet the delivery of her excuse did not ring true. She was slightly giggly as if there were someone there not just listening but almost egging her on. He thought about it all night and hardly slept as a result, and was very crabby the next day when he saw her in the office.

When she walked in, he could not help but notice she was unusually wearing a colourful but flimsy chiffon scarf which she had presumably donned to hide what looked like a faint love bite on her neck. She was evasive, too, and could not look him in the eye... So what were those protestations of love all about, which she had proclaimed only a few days before? He could get nothing but obfuscation and denial out of her, so, confused and depressed, he was glad of a number of meetings he had to attend which, for once, did not concern her. They were boring but better than being in the same office with her – yet his attention wandered and on two occasions knew he had missed the point being made by the speaker and had to bluster an answer in response. He found himself wishing he had never walked out on Berenice and he found his mind kept reverting back to that unexpected and wonderful evening with her. Well, at least it had ended well – for her, at least. How he still loved her, though…

When he eventually returned to the office, Lin Yang was not there so he got down to his work and hardly noticed when she returned.

"Hello," she said simply but directly.

He looked up. "Hello, darling," he replied pointedly.

This threw Lin Yang off her guard for an instant. "Sorry about last night," she mumbled, "but—"

"So who is he?" Shuo asked, not looking away from his screen.

This confounded her: he had taken control of the situation and turned it into a minor inquisition. Her thoughts and emotions were suddenly scrambled. So she did what she often did with him in awkward emotional situations and burst into tears. But the usual comforting arm around her shoulder and soft kiss were not forthcoming this time. Instead, he just looked up and coldly observed her.

He knew. But how? It was women who always knew when men were having affairs, seldom the other way around. She did not know where to look or where to go but swept out of the office wrapped in a damp cloud of guilt.

Chapter Thirty-Two

—⟋⟍—

What had happened the night before had been resisted for all the right reasons and succumbed to for all the wrong ones. Before Berenice's unnoticed witnessing of events, Lin Yang had had every intention of going back to Shuo in his flat. But she suddenly found herself incapable of leaving Berndt: he was sexy in a muted way and had a way with English words which she desperately wanted to know better, even if she did not fully understand them. Above all, she loved his voice, which was soothing and relaxing. His laugh, too, was like gravel coated with honey, and after the first kiss – the one Berenice had seen – she could not bear to leave him. They had stood outside the café for some time debating what should happen next, with her knowing she should go and him underlining the fact he was only there for one more day before leaving. That had been the rub: it is one thing to know you like someone but another to be forced into a situation which you believe is inevitable but needs time to progress. He had even walked away when she had decided to go home to Shuo – she had talked about him much early on as an insurance policy but less and less as the evening progressed – only to find herself running after Berndt with a look in her eye that said 'Yes' without actually ever saying it.

And so it was that she had found herself in his hotel room being plied with drinks from the mini-bar and sitting – then, indiscreetly soon, lying on – the bed, with various items of clothing finding themselves on the floor. He had not forced her – cajoled was a better word – and soon he was inside her, driving her into eruptions of delight. When it was all over and Berndt had gone to the bathroom, she suddenly found herself consumed by guilt – but acknowledged with a discreet smile that he was even better at it than Shuo. Shuo had been a revelation but Berndt was majestic in his foreplay and ultimate consummation of the act, which she put down to his being older and more experienced. Then she wondered if she would just be the latest in a long line of many others and found herself longing to get back to the safety of Shuo. *A bit late, mind you*, she admitted. Was every pretty girl's life this complicated? Or was Berndt the 'one' and really the decent, caring, lovely man she was hoping him to be? Only time would tell, but that was pressing: in the meantime she had to go back to a relationship with Shuo while Berndt went back to Sweden. The cart before the horse? No, she concluded: sometimes you have to grasp the moment – and that was what it had been.

Another aspect which had warmed her to Berndt was that, when her guilt had become insuperable, he had left the room so she could chat privately with Shuo to say she was back in her flat feeling ill and could not see him that night; Berndt had let her talk for a minute or two before looking round the door and making silly faces, which had made her giggle. Then he had returned to the bathroom but listened at its door and smiled to himself: he really did like her and would be back in Beijing to see her as soon as his business trips permitted. In the meantime, she could sort herself out with Shuo and he would come back to a free woman.

Of that, he was arrogantly certain.

—⁓—

Berenice went to the studios early the next morning, still anxious about her predicament and wondering when her results would come back. Her designs were a blur in front of her and when the head designer came for a discussion to see how she was getting on and was there anything he could explain or help her with, she was glad of the distraction. Five more days and George would be back: it was certainly cutting it fine.

She went back to her desk after lunch, much bolstered by the praise that her department head had bestowed upon her; almost everyone seemed to know who she was and the reflected respect they had for George was like a cloak of confidence around her. Many of them seemed to sense she was pregnant, too, which made her proud, happy – and safe from predators. But she was still somewhat concerned.

It would be a long few days.

—⁓—

It was evening and Shuo faced Lin Yang in his flat. She knew they had to have a confrontation but certainly did not want to do so at work, where the likes of the prowling Natalya would use it as a stick to imply their private lives were taking over their jobs. Lin Yang had proclaimed that she did not want him to go to her flat because she had left in a rush that morning and it was a mess – which Shuo reluctantly accepted but which also added to his suspicions. She had spoken to Berndt that morning after Shuo's confrontation and it had been clear she was emotional – but he had decided to take an earlier flight and was already in the airport departure lounge so could not talk openly or for long. From being on top of everything and having believed she and Shuo would make a go of their relationship and settle down, she had allowed herself to be seduced by a complete stranger as a way – she realised – of justifying her superiority. And now she had betrayed her previous intended and made him deeply upset as well as not knowing whether she would ever see Berndt again. Oh, what had she done?

So she tried the tears again but Shuo was unmoved; he just kept asking what had happened, and who with… so she eventually told him.

He just sat there, his head in his hands, not weeping but visibly shocked. Yet inside, he knew he had no justification for admonishing her after what he had done with Berenice. It was human nature to find people attractive and sometimes it went too far. Nonetheless, he found himself enjoying the moral superiority because she did not know about that: Lin Yang had certainly suspected him of an indiscretion but despite her probing he had never admitted it. And, anyway, he justified to himself, his was a termination of a previous long-term relationship, not what was probably a one-night stand. An end, rather than a beginning.

Armed with this moral rectitude, he rang for a taxi and asked her to take her things and leave. It was only as she stood sobbing at the door that he found some compassion and put his arm around her, but he was resolute: her actions had done him a favour and he had suddenly discovered his inner man. The situation might be resolvable, but he would need some assurance from her: lots of it. And what Berndt and she did or did not do next would be crucial. He was her superior at the office, too, even if he had given her the prime spot there to boost her confidence after Berenice's departure. But now it was his turn: through the adversity of love he had found himself and, as the door closed, he suddenly felt a power he had never experienced before.

And just as the two women in his life had, he was really enjoying it.

Chapter Thirty-Three

—␣ᄿ␣—

It is a truism to say that love conquers all but, due to its errant influences, the next few months would determine the path in life of each protagonist in very different ways…

The day before George returned, Berenice had received her DNA test results. She had trembled as she opened the package, terrified at what a Pandora's Box she might be unleashing: yet the result was negative – the baby must be George's! Relieved and emotional, she burst into tears but could not tell anyone except Shuo. Yet that would be… well, an insult, wouldn't it? Of course he had to know if he was the father or not; so it was doubly important to tell him that the child was not his. He would, of course, have hoped it was, in a way – so creating a lifelong link between them, a mutual secret that no-one else could know; but that might have bred resentment, court cases, ill-feeling and future rancour. So how fortunate she was that nothing could now be held against her that might split her from George. Yes, she had to tell him he was not the father.

When she rang to tell him, he sounded down, which she initially mistook for his wishing the child had been his; but when the more immediate reason was known – his split from Lin Yang – she almost wished she had not told him at all, for his sake, not hers. Apart from glimpsing Lin Yang in the café with an unknown man, and Shuo briefly in the ice-cream parlour, she had not seen them for a while and at that time they had seemed to be getting on well. She did not want to tell him what she had seen – that was none of her business; but nonetheless wanted to say something to make him feel better. As they spoke, the sadness in his voice began to affect her and she became very aware of how fond he had been of Lin Yang, so ejecting her from his life was of huge disappointment to him. She resisted the temptation to ask if she would like him to go round to comfort him as that would upset him further – of that she was certain. So she just kept talking to him... and realised again what a good and influential person he had been for both her and Lin Yang: he did not deserve this pain. They finished the call and afterwards she shed a tear for the man who had been her friend and confidant for such an important time in her life. But for now there was nothing else she could do.

—ɷ—

Lin Yang looked at herself in the mirror and – noting the tearful, bloodshot eyes, runny nose and dishevelled hair – came to the conclusion that she had been very cruel. Shuo had given her a wonderful job – as he had done to Berenice before him – and she had benefited from his kindness and sexual awakening; yet she had then kicked him in the teeth on a whim and reduced him to a husk. Where was her honour? She tried to argue that she could not help finding Berndt attractive, worldly and sexy, but still had not heard from him since he left; so had she thrown all the good things with Shuo away for nothing? And how difficult would it be in the office together from now on? She had not even admitted to everything – there was no need. She had made her deceit so obvious. Now both of them were in different flats and she had lost a potential husband and father. A 'ping' from her phone momentarily intruded on her feelings of despair but she disregarded the text as her dislike for herself grew. Then, with a new torrent of tears, she threw herself on her bed and cried for another hour before falling into a tormented sleep.

When she eventually woke and looked at her phone, she found that the text was from Berndt, who had arrived home safely and wanted to talk. Immediately, her countenance and mood improved dramatically and was so relieved he had got in touch that she decided to videocall him. But not yet; she had to make herself look – and feel – better before she could do that.

Standing naked in the shower, she started to re-acquire her confidence and stopped castigating herself over her actions; Shuo was a boy and Berndt was a man. And after drying her hair and putting on a revealing top and some make-up, she was ready to call him. And Shuo suddenly seemed even further away emotionally than Berndt was geographically…

—w—

A few days later at the airport, George threw his arms around Berenice and they kissed as wildly as their personal discretion allowed. Once in the car, though, they didn't notice the surroundings, the traffic, the metallic skies and the looks of opprobrium from George's driver at all.

Despite his feeling of release, Shuo sat in his office, a despondent, broken man. He had loved Berenice and failed; as a result of ditching her, he had acquired another beauty whom he had fallen in love with – and now failed with her, too. He had given a lift up to both of these women and yet they seemed to resent him for it. Where was he going wrong? He had not seen Lin Yang that morning and, bearing in mind that he was still technically her boss, had tried to ascertain where she was – only to find that she had blocked him from her phone. He had looked at her diary, too, to see if she was at a meeting, but there were no appointments there until the afternoon. Was she at home, regretting what had happened but afraid to lose face by coming back to the office?

In fact, what he did not know was that she had come in very early and waited for Mr. Chen to arrive, whereupon she had explained to him that she and Shuo had fallen out and could she move to another office, please? Chen was visibly surprised and not a little upset by this – not just from a personal level but also because he felt their relationship had been very constructive, business having significantly improved in their department over the past few weeks. So what would happen to their steady and often strikingly good growth curve? How would they interact now? Lin Yang had unexpectedly said a few unkind things about Shuo, such as that he was uninspiring and often resisted new ideas to help growth and efficiency: this was untrue and Mr. Chen knew it, but he could not bring himself to say so. Lin Yang was so beautiful and had become a woman rather than the girl who had started only a few months before: she had done well. But he also knew that this was down to Shuo and could not help but think she had used him: so he would not accede to her request – they would have to sort it out together and she must go back to the office and make it work. As she left, he pondered the insinuations and decided to get Shuo's side of the story.

So when Lin Yang arrived back in Shuo's presence, she was not in the best of humours – and Shuo knew her well enough not to probe. She just walked past him and, shutting her door – what should have been *his* door! – went straight to her computer. A few minutes later, he received a call from Natalya asking him to come up and see Mr. Chen as soon as possible.

"So what's going on?" Chen asked, as he motioned Shuo to sit down.

Shuo, not having known of Lin Yang's earlier presence in the boss's office, was confused; had Mr. Chen observed a rift between them? Or Natalya, who would revel in fabricating dirt on them? Or had he done something wrong professionally?

"I'm sorry, Mr. Chen: I don't know what you're referring to."

After a moment staring at him, Mr. Chen just said, "You and Lin Yang."

Ah, that was it. So who had told him? With a pained realisation, Shuo concluded that it could only have been Lin Yang. "I thought our relationship was a private matter," he said guardedly.

"Indeed it is; but Lin Yang was up here a few minutes ago asking if she could have a separate office from you."

Shuo was shocked, then furious. "She asked that?" he retorted.

Mr. Chen nodded in such a way as to imply he did not know whose side to take.

After a moment, Shuo, who had looked around the room as if trying to find inspiration for an answer, then faced Mr. Chen, took a deep breath, and said: "She's found someone else and gone off with him. I have not done anything wrong. It's her choice but, as you can imagine, I'm somewhat upset. And, if you must know, annoyed, too; we had a wonderful relationship both at work and in our private lives, and now she's blaming me for her falling for someone else."

"She says you started an affair with Berenice again."

That went like a crossbow bolt to his heart and his anger intensified: Lin Yang did not know that. "No, I did not," he blurted. "Berenice and I remained friends, even if things were difficult after I met Lin Yang because Berenice was my first true love – until recently, anyway." He held the bridge of his nose and closed his eyes as he tried to suppress a tear of emotion and, yes, fury, then took a deep sigh and continued, "But that's over, she's gone – and marrying an Englishman, too. *And* she's pregnant by him." That last sentence was said with added inflection as it was the one thing Shuo knew he could get away with – thanks to his recent subterfuge. "And I just have to accept that Lin Yang doesn't want me any more but it won't spoil our business relationship, I assure you – at least as far as I'm concerned."

Mr. Chen stood up, came around his desk and patted Shuo on the shoulder, then just stood there, unsure what to do. He liked Shuo and thought well of his business capabilities but he did not think that Lin Yang would let it go, and that was bad for the department. "Go and sort it out," he said kindly, and went back to his desk.

Shuo took his cue to leave, motivated by a desire to have a blazing row with Lin Yang and noticing, as he passed Natalya, that there was a smug grin on her face.

He reached the office and walked straight in, opening the door into Lin Yang's as she stood up – as if retreating into the wall – and let rip. It was the first time in his life he had ever dressed down a junior – yes, she *was* his junior, despite him making her feel more important by offering her the largesse of his office she was sitting in – and said everything he had to say. She stood in terror as he countered and dismissed the accusations she had levelled at him through Mr. Chen but tempered the volume in a controlled and dignified way.

He did not give her the chance to reply, either, so after demanding she gave him back his office, he slammed the door and sat at his desk which would hitherto be Lin Yang's. He then started gathering up his things in anticipation of returning to his true office but noticed that Natalya must have witnessed much of the episode as he saw her slinking away. What a witch that woman was!

Looking back at Lin Yang, he noticed she was in tears, her face white with fear and resentment, but on the phone to someone. *Must be her lover*, he thought with disdain. *Well, good luck to both of them.* And he left the room.

Chapter Thirty-Four

—⁊⁊⁊—

Things moved very swiftly after these events. Natalya had, of course, witnessed the tirade Shuo had fired at Lin Yang and exaggerated his anger as she recounted her observations to Mr. Chen. In turn, Mr. Chen had mentioned the episode to the chairman during business prattle but – despite assuring him that all would be well as a result of creative tension – the chairman was less forgiving and had told him to sack Shuo immediately for harassment. Mr. Chen resisted but the chairman was adamant: he had always disliked Shuo. Perhaps, also, he was envious of his ability to find beautiful young women with heads for business. Yet with that brutal instruction, it had made Mr. Chen wonder whether Lin Yang had been quietly ingratiating herself with him: so he asked the one person he loathed in the company, his assistant, Natalya, whether Lin Yang had been seeing the chairman more than necessary and she, keen to finish off the young lothario, had said, "Yes." Mr. Chen did not believe her, of course; he knew she just loved sowing discord – but he had to accept it might be true, whether he doubted her or no.

So Lin Yang stayed in her office and, after Shuo had departed, took on a young man whom she tormented mercilessly as if out of spite or a substitute for what she could never have done to Shuo; in fact, deep down, she fully admitted to herself that it was resentment at Shuo throwing her out that drove this festering anger within her but that it was all her own fault: she had sacrificed a good man for a silly indiscretion and knew her rage was due to her own poor behaviour.

To make matters worse, she had never heard from Berndt again, either.

—◊—

So while Berenice continued to do well in her new life, Shuo descended into a state of depression and self-loathing.

Lin Yang had, indeed, been ingratiating herself with the chairman as much as she was able: the cheery wave when they were on opposing sides of the room, the odd request for advice regarding a business matter – which would have infuriated Mr. Chen had he known – sitting in the front row when there were company meetings, where she would cross and uncross her stockinged legs, and many other subtle (and not so subtle) wiles she had discovered she was capable of. She had Shuo to thank for these – he was always so receptive to her sexy ways that she had become an expert in alluring provocation.

Now that she was running her department under Mr. Chen, she realised that, should she become his assistant, she could get even closer to the chairman. Yet that would mean dislodging Natalya, which would be difficult. Natalya knew everyone and everything, which was why she had managed to stay in her position for so long. Yet it was so obvious that Mr. Chen loathed her that Yang wondered whether it was because she had something over Mr. Chen – or even the chairman – neither of whom could allow her to be sacked. But what was it? If it was a misdemeanour from Mr. Chen, Natalya would have managed his dismissal years ago, so it could not be that. It must be the chairman, then. She suspected he had mistresses – she had guessed that long ago – but that at least meant she might be able to turn his eye in her direction much more easily. Natalya would not talk to her, of course, so there was no mileage to be gained there; but if she could imply Natalya had been doing something wrong, then she might be able to get rid of this reviled woman that way. If she could, she knew she would be liked by everyone: in fact, she felt it would not only be a very good thing for her, but also Mr. Chen. And just about everyone else in the company, too.

So, not for the first time, she decided that someone had to go – Natalya.

A few days later, she had to see Mr. Chen about an issue of non-payment from a supplier and made an appointment. At the prescribed time, she arrived at his office to find neither he nor Natalya were there. Being alone, she remembered that, on a previous occasion when Mr. Chen had been out of his office, she had come across Natalya unexpectedly and had seen her leafing furtively through what she knew were expenses sheets on her desk, which were a dull yellow colour; on seeing Lin Yang, Natalya had somewhat quickly and clumsily stuffed them into her drawer, slamming it shut with uncharacteristic speed, as if she were trying to hide something. It had not meant much to Yang at the time, but being in the empty office, the incident suddenly came back to her. What if Natalya was fiddling her expenses?

An idea came into her mind, but she had to act quickly: her desire to be rid of this woman for her own advancement suddenly trumped her concerns about being caught, so she quickly went around the desk and opened the appropriate drawer. Instinctively, she delved to the bottom and found what appeared to be some papers like those she had witnessed Natalya stuffing into the drawer before, quickly taking them out and hiding them in another folder she had with her. She could return them later after Natalya had gone home. And even if Natalya realised they had been taken and she was indeed doing something wrong, then she could not tell anyone!

Lin Yang closed the drawer and quickly returned to the seat opposite the desk, nonchalantly awaiting Mr. Chen's arrival. He did so a few minutes later and they swiftly concluded the meeting. Natalya had arrived a few minutes after Mr. Chen but was seemingly unaware of the theft which had just taken place as Yang left, she only being subjected to the customary frosty stare.

Back in her office, she closed the door and discreetly looked at the expense sheets. They were dynamite: obviously believing she was above suspicion or knew too much about too many people whom she could blackmail, Natalya had been somewhat insouciant about keeping these papers properly hidden.

But from Lin Yang's perspective, there was now possibly a chance to destroy her...

—⁓—

Natalya locked her drawers and went home. Not long after, Lin Yang was in Mr. Chen's office and putting the files, sealed in a strong, thick plastic envelope, on his desk, with a computer-typed printout adhered to the top which simply read: "Private – for Mr. Chen's eyes only. Highly sensitive." She had not applied her name to any part of the package, but Natalya's was all over the sheets inside and appeared to show she was embezzling money on behalf of the finance director and the CEO.

Yang left, knowing Mr. Chen always came in early and would see the files long before Natalya. She also had a copy of them in her bag, which she would keep at home, just in case…

The next morning, she came in to find a note on her desk from Mr. Chen, asking him to come and see him immediately. She did.

Natalya greeted her with the usual dismissive stare, which relieved Yang as it meant Natalya had no idea what she had come to see Mr. Chen about. Mr. Chen saw her and came out of his office to intercept her, with the opened envelope under his arm; shepherding her away from the toxicity of his assistant and away into the boardroom, he firmly closed the door behind them and locked it. He was slightly breathless and had a worried look on his face. He came straight to the point.

"Where did you find these files?" he asked in a hushed tone, as if he were concerned the room might be bugged.

"In Natalya's drawer," Yang replied.

He looked shocked. "What were you doing looking in

there?" he enquired, even more worried, and as if he did not really want to believe her.

Lin Yang explained the reasons she had become suspicious of Natalya, adding at the end that if the files could be substantiated then Mr. Chen could be rid of her.

Chen looked at her momentarily, raised an eyebrow and looked back at the files, emitting an, "I wish," under his breath. Then he turned back to her and quietly said, "These could destroy not just her but the CEO *and* the finance director. You appreciate that?"

Yang nodded but said nothing.

He then looked back at the files, opening them only slightly as if terrified some other dreadful disclosure might pop out.

"I shall have to see the chairman," he said gravely. "Would you mind coming with me? He likes you. More than me, anyway..."

Yang gave him a quizzical glance and then nodded again. "I think it would be a good idea," she concurred.

Mr. Chen looked at her, obviously thinking that she was doing this for herself as well as him, and stood up. "I hope the chairman isn't part of this too," he said with a nervous smile, "or we'll both be for the chop, too."

Lin Yang nodded once more: that thought had also crossed her mind...

"Let's go *now*," he said, with a sudden air of resolution, "before that woman finds out these are missing. And before I lose my will to go through with this."

They left the boardroom, sailed past the startled Natalya and took the lift to the top floor. A few moments later, they were shown into the chairman's expansive office and Mr.

Chen noted that the man they had come to see was far more interested in Lin Yang than himself: Lin's inclusion had been a good ploy to arrest the chairman's attention – as long as he was not too distracted from the serious issue at stake.

Chen described the issue and then put the files on the chairman's desk as he finished the charges, as if emphasising the point. The chairman listened and looked dispassionate as the nub of the charges was laid. Mr. Chen was already sweating: this could turn back to bite him, he knew. Natalya had been placed in the position by senior forces, which included high-ranking government personnel…

The chairman leafed through the papers with a kind of superior disdain, which made even Lin Yang wonder whether he was in collusion with the scam and that she, too, might soon be out of the company with no references.

There was a nasty silence, then the chairman's brow furrowed and he looked more closely at one of the entries. He began to look very angry – he had seen something which obviously struck a chord – and he blew vehemently through his teeth, throwing the papers down onto his desk and getting up. He turned to the window, shoved his hands in his pockets and stared out across the skyscape for a few moments before sitting back at the table, rubbing his fat fingers into his cheeks and letting out another sigh of disbelief. Then he turned to Mr. Chen and Lin Yang. "Thank you for bringing this to my attention… this goes to the very top… and I don't just mean here. It also explains many things, such as why our profits are not as we expected them to be. Let's just say that there's been a leak in the waterworks, for want of a good expression…" He then turned to Lin Yang and said, "Thank you, too, Lin

Yang; you have shown great courage in bringing this to our attention. Heads are going to roll. Mr. Chen – it must have been a difficult decision to let Lin Yang bring this to me, too, but... Well, between you and me, I know that Natalya is poison and you've wanted to get rid of her for years... so did I, actually. But there were 'people' who wanted her to stay. Now I know why. I'll fire her immediately. And if there are, shall we say, 'higher repercussions', then I will stand by you. Please send Natalya up to me now. I shall get rid of her as soon as she steps into this room. As far as I can see, she doesn't have a leg to stand on."

With that, he waved them away, and two very relieved and vindicated people walked out of the chairman's office...

Outside, Mr. Chen told Lin Yang to go directly back to her office as he did not want to risk the blame for Natalya's demise to be visited upon her: he would have great pleasure in telling her to go to see the chairman immediately. Just before they parted, though, he called Lin Yang back and told her that, should she wish to have Natalya's job helping him run the department, it was hers – starting today, if she wanted it. *That's a good start*, thought Lin Yang as she accepted, then turned away with a smirk on her face and descended the stairs to ensure no meeting with the disgraced Natalya was likely; her high heels' clicking noise resonated around the empty stairwell as if implying a spatial void which she was now in a position to fill. *Step one accomplished*, she mused; *now to work on step two – the chairman's office.*

Before Natalya would suffer the chairman's wrath, he made a number of calls to top government officials and told his PA to summon the finance director and CEO to the office at the same time – that was, now.

Natalya arrived first and was asked to wait outside; as first the CEO and then the finance director arrived, she became very worried – which was just what the chairman had intended. The finance director realised something was up when the CEO arrived too and, although he looked nervous and started to sweat, the CEO obviously thought himself above whatever the chairman had summoned them for and continued sending emails on his phone until they were all called in together. Then, when the charges were laid against them all, he was as worried as the others.

The meeting was over within twenty minutes and three ashen, admonished executives walked silently out of the office, then the building and out into the wider world. They were all finished. An hour later, Lin Yang was sitting in Natalya's chair outside Mr. Chen's office and its previous occupant was nowhere to be seen. The only communication she had with the previous incumbent was a vicious email with a number of pernicious and very unpleasant insults, which Lin Yang deleted. She never heard from Natalya again.

Epilogue

—⁂—

After the upheavals at the company, the revelations from Lin Yang's actions had led to the uncovering of more illicit dealings – indeed, hers were only the tip of a rather large iceberg. However, after top-down inquiries – and more sackings of senior personnel – the company recovered quickly and started to do well without these financial improprieties holding up its growth. Yet it was true to say that no-one, except the disgraced players, had ever noticed. So without Natalya as gatekeeper to the subterfuge, Mr. Chen's department became far more immersed in the greater functioning of the enterprise and thus attracted more conducive people and better cross-fertilisation of ideas than the fierce presence of Natalya had hitherto allowed. Lin Yang's stock had never been higher. Conversely, Shuo was not missed or even much remembered – except by Mr. Chen, who would forever be appalled at his dismissal by the chairman.

Yet he was soon to be appalled again: after a few weeks sorting out his own office, the chairman – no doubt with

the connivance and heightened influence of Lin Yang –
offered this lady the job as his new PA when the current
one retired in a few months' time. If she wanted it. She did,
of course: and with neither Shuo nor Berndt in her life
any more she realised she could gain even more power by
becoming the chairman's mistress, too; to say this was very
much appreciated would be to underestimate his libidinous
predilections, and he submitted easily to her approaches.
This achieved, she used all her new resources to become
an avaricious predator: she saw that she could eventually
run the company if she found all the skeletons in his and
the other board members' cupboards and, thus, become
the powerful woman she had only recently wished to be,
motivated by greed, spite, revenge and ambition – a far cry
from the somewhat gauche and naïve young girl whom
Shuo had first met only a year or so before... To an astute
observer, she had become a second Natalya – albeit far
more physically attractive.

Berenice and George's marriage ceremony had gone
beautifully well and the pregnancy she had worried about
soon manifested itself as a daughter, whom they called
Marika. As the girl grew up, it became obvious to Berenice
that she had a strange resemblance to Shuo but kidded
herself that it must just be coincidence...

But the doubt persisted over the years and one day,
when George was in England, she looked up Shuo's number
and found herself talking to him. It had been over seven
years since they last spoke and so much had happened: she
had not only produced Marika but a little boy whom they
named Xiao Jhong, who looked far more Western than
Marika ever would.

George was producing shows all over China, the United States and Great Britain, and she saw him fleetingly, he was so busy; she had stayed at the TV company but also gone freelance as her set designs had been feted – and she had even designed some shows in London one time. She loved going to England and spoke to Shuo wistfully of the beautiful house they had re-furbished to her tastes in Wiltshire.

Whilst Berenice was telling Shuo all about what had happened in her life since they had lost contact, she was intrigued by the fact that Shuo would say little of what had happened to him: he hinted that he did not work for the company where they had first met but declined to say more until or unless he could speak to her face to face; so they arranged to meet at the Summer Palace for a talk about old times, which they both felt would be a revealing and friendly thing to do.

It was a beautiful summer's day and the blossoms were in sharp contrast to the deep blue sky which, in itself, was such an unusual occurrence in Beijing. She recognised Shuo from afar: he had hardly changed but had put on a little weight, which suited him and, although his boyish air had matured, he still looked young and was consequently better-looking than when she had known him all those years ago. It appeared he had acquired a certain gravitas, too, which she found attractive before she even started talking to him.

It seemed that the actual passage of years was far less than in reality and they fell into conversation easily, as ex-lovers often do when the pain of misunderstandings, angry words and resentments have disappeared into the relative mists of time. Before long, they found a bench near the white jade boat moored permanently on the lake, sat down and started to talk.

"So what are you doing, now?" Berenice enquired. "You seem so loath to tell me."

"It's a long story," he replied, defensively.

"Oh, go on. I mean, did you marry Lin Yang, for example?"

He took a deep sigh, looked into the far distance across the lake beyond the boat, towards the distant bridge, and began.

"Soon after you and I last met, I found that Lin Yang was having an affair. I don't know who it was or when it started, but it became obvious."

Berenice raised an eyebrow but kept quiet on what she had seen herself so let him continue.

"When I challenged her, she wouldn't admit it, but she didn't deny it either, so I just knew. Then she admitted it, so I finished with her. I felt that, if I couldn't even discuss what might have been wrong with our relationship, then there was no point in continuing. She got very emotional and angry and basically lost the plot. So I left. The morning after, she wasn't in the office and there was nothing in her diary so I was sure she was avoiding me. And in a sense, she was: she was with Mr. Chen, saying that we had fallen out and that she wanted to be in a different office as she couldn't work with me any more, as if it was my fault. Well, Mr. Chen took my side but by then I think Lin Yang had been finding ways of making the chairman notice her and so when Chen discussed it with him, instead of telling Lin Yang to respect me, he ordered Chen to fire me. So I was pushed out."

Berenice was visibly shaken by this news; she knew how much Shuo had loved his job, and Lin Yang, too – although never as much as he had loved her: that had come out during their night of abandon. But she stayed quiet to let his tale evolve.

"I was given two months' salary, so I wasn't financially distressed for a while as I looked for another job – but it became difficult. Then, just as I was getting desperate, I received a call from Lin Yang's previous company—"

"You mean, the one she left to come to our company?"

He nodded. "Yes; I didn't know the guy but he said he'd heard about me from someone else and he'd like to interview me. They'd had some investment and were looking for someone to take them a stage further."

"And that 'someone else' was Lin Yang, you think?"

"Yes. I think she realised how she had betrayed me, stitched me up, hurt me, and felt bad about it; a lover's last act of compassion to a soul she'd broken." He paused and looked at Berenice, as if to imply that she had broken his soul, too. Then he turned away and, looking again into the distance, resumed. "By the way, as you know, I *had* made her pregnant," he added, then gave her a look and smiled wistfully. "I always wished more that *your* child had been mine, though..."

Berenice shuddered; was he going to ask her what even she believed might be the truth? And would it matter now, anyway, if she said she was not sure? She knew Shuo would not tell George – he had undergone too much pain and would not inflict it upon her. So, should she voice her doubts about the DNA test, with Marika looking so like the man she was now talking to?

No: despite an urge to admit to Shuo her suspicions, it would be worse for him if he knew there was even a faint possibility: he would want to see the child and then George would want to know who this man was and… No; the possible truth could be too awkward and might cause terrible ructions.

Yet the fact that he saw her finding it difficult to respond made him persist: "It was mine, wasn't it?"

There was the Shuo she had known before: sometimes challenging her sense of control. But she had mellowed, too, and so she just looked at him and, due to her internal quandaries, just said, "I don't want to say any more."

"But I do."

She found herself going pink, which was nothing to do with the weather but her own embarrassment. "All right: it wasn't yours, as I told you – you gave me the swab and I checked the paternity. It was George's."

A smile crept across Shuo's face.

"Why are you smirking?" she asked nervously.

He just looked at her, then, with an impish smile: "I don't want to say any more." As her curiosity was something she had conjectured herself, she became more desperate to know what he was hiding from her, so decided to tease it from him and said, "I have to admit that Marika does look like you: she has your eyes and looks totally Chinese…" She looked at him and saw a tear welling in his eye: he knew something she did not.

"Marika," he said. "A girl." He blotted his now very moist eyes on his sleeve and turned away, muttering, "What a lovely name, too."

Berenice suddenly wondered if she had ascertained the

truth she had not dared to expect: had it not been Shuo's DNA but someone else's? He was by now so overcome with emotion – she could hear little sobs coming from his direction even though she could not see the tears. In an instant she realised she would have to forgive him if she was to know the likely truth. Strangely, she was not angry but touched.

"Shuo," she said, trying to get him to look at her. "Even if you did deceive me, I won't hold it against you."

He turned, the tears streaming down his face.

"Did you give me someone else's DNA on that swab?" He looked at her and then the flood broke through as he nodded, throwing his arms around her and holding her close to him as her blouse became drenched in warm tears. "I'm so sorry," he said. "But I did it for you. If it had been proved to be my child, then you would have found it so hard to appease George and I didn't want you to be hurt, so..." He tailed off.

A huge well of emotion, relief and even happiness swept over Berenice. And as Shuo cried on her shoulder, she suddenly knew that she had achieved all that she wanted: a beautiful girl by the Chinese boy she had once loved but resisted, and a son from her English husband who would give them both so much joy as well. It was all so strangely perfect. As long as Shuo did not tell anyone.

When she asked, he shook his head and mumbled, "Of course not – I still love you too much to do that." Then he added, "It's our secret."

"So whose DNA did you give me?"

He shrugged – he did not know; a Westerner, probably American. And he told her what had happened. At the end, she found herself smiling: Shuo had done something terrible but wonderful and she knew once more why she had loved him when she did – even if she had not fully appreciated him at the time.

The sun was setting and a chill had descended on the palace grounds, so they made their way to a small restaurant and continued their discussions. Shuo had cleverly still not divulged any information about himself and so she was keen to find out who was in his life now.

The restaurant was quite empty and it was possible to talk without being overheard. So she looked at him and quite simply asked him that question. The reply surprised her.

In England, George was trying to get in touch with Berenice but could not get through. He had been working hard and the constant flying, meetings, creative energy, aftermath of divorce and having two young children had been getting to him, despite his blissful happiness with his new wife. So much so that, one evening during a recording in Manchester, he had suddenly suffered chest pains and had been rushed to hospital. He had not told Berenice and – being in a private ward – had managed to avoid the necessity of telling her: she would have dropped everything if he had, he knew – to the possible detriment of their children's education – and, as he was told he would recover, decided to just talk to her without the usual video and say he was fine.

He managed to keep this façade up for a few days until he left the hospital but realised that he was very tired and could not keep up his hectic schedule – at least not without a few weeks' rest. That being anathema to him, he soldiered on and brushed aside his problem as a 'minor issue'. He certainly did not want to become a passenger on his own shows so kept up the pretence of being well as best he could. Yet the constant fatigue was debilitating and eventually he informed his many clients that he would be taking a few weeks off; he told Berenice he would be coming back to Beijing in a few days' time, whereupon they could go on holiday somewhere warm and luxurious to unwind and relax.

Yet at about the same time as Berenice was talking to Shuo, his fragile body was having other ideas…

—∽—

"I have no-one in my life," Shuo confessed embarrassedly. "I loved you and you caused me to leave you; I then met Lin Yang and she met someone else… and then decided to become the chairman's mistress rather than stay with me, and so I just sort of lost my confidence. I've seen a few girls but… it's not the same as with either of you."

"But you are still working, aren't you?" Berenice enquired, touched but concerned and fearing the answer might be negative.

"Oh, yes – I'm still working at Lin Yang's previous company. I enjoy it. It's going places and I'm now the second in command. But I can't fulfil my life properly without someone to love… But I just find it… illusory, now."

She touched his arm and a thrill went up it, just as it had always done. Some things never change. Yet they were about to…

After they had finished their meal, they said fond farewells and she took a taxi home. She felt sorry for him and her part in his disillusion, but there was no way she could change the past and, as the traffic, flyovers, underpasses, offices and tower blocks flashed past her in the gathering gloom, she felt so glad she had George – her rock, her husband and father to her children. Well, one of them anyway. As she thought this, her phone suddenly found a signal and sprung into life: it was George.

—∞—

Shuo went home and spent the rest of the evening in a state of recrimination. He blamed himself for everything that had gone wrong in his love life, and although he knew that it was all over with Berenice, at least he had regained her trust and friendship. And she knew his secret. He was surprised she had not seemed affected by the news and surmised she had half expected it to come out at some point – but he was still glad she had not been angry. That would have made him even more depressed. So it was all out in the open now and that was that. He poured himself another drink and watched the television, falling asleep in front of it and waking in the small hours with a raging headache. He picked up his phone from the hallway as he struggled towards the bedroom and realised there was a message there. It was from Berenice. Expecting that it was just her thanking him for a nice evening and it had been good to meet again, he did not read it and went to bed. When he woke up, it was a long time later but he was thrown into life when he read it: she needed him – for all the wrong reasons.

He rang her immediately and found himself instantly involved in a terrible and very personal tragedy...

—⁓—

When Berenice had taken George's call in the taxi, it had not been him on the phone but a doctor from a hospital in London with the terrible news that George had passed away in the mid-morning of a heart attack: it had originally been treatable but he had suddenly acquired complications and they got him into theatre too late to save him; Berenice was a widow.

She was devastated. Her whole life had gone the way she'd created it and this terrible shock was the first time it had been disrupted; her darling George, the liberator of her soul, desires and aspirations, who had paved her pathway to happiness, was no more. He had been her beacon, giving her new insights into art, music, confidence, wealth, self-importance, the meaning of life itself... and his presence would always be with her despite now never being able to see him again. How could he do this to her? Why had he not taken more care of himself? And, yet, that was the George she loved – living life to the full, exposing beauty, trust and possibilities as easily as turning on a tap: how was she going to live without him? Yes, she should not have enticed Shuo into that night of lust and wonder, but that was her way of closing a door which had been left ajar. She had had to assert her control – yet now all vestige of that control had been ripped from her with the death of the one man who had ever truly understood her – in truth, the love of her life.

She had arrived back to their flat whence she first told the maid and then her two children what had happened – and then suffered their anguish and tears as well as trying to control her own. Being the elder, Marika was the one who felt it most, while Xiao Jhong was more bewildered than upset until the despair of his mother and sister got to him too. She had called the only other person she could trust, but he had not answered; why was he not there for her when she needed him?

Yet by the time Shuo rang next morning, the maid told him Berenice was asleep and she would get her to call him later – but he should be prepared for the fact she had some devastating news to impart. This had thrown Shuo into turmoil: what devastating news? Was she ill? Had one of her children been diagnosed with something terrible? Was his daughter, Marika, all right? Yet the one thing that never crossed his mind was that something awful had happened to George…

He had a shower and readied himself for her call, when he could then offer her a shoulder to cry on, whatever it was. And he knew that – after George – he was probably the best person to do this… So when Berenice did eventually ring, he was completely caught out by her news – the more so for its complete unexpectedness. Being so attuned to Berenice and still loving her so much, it hurt him deeply, and he instinctively understood what she was experiencing. He immediately offered his presence, however meagre a solace, but which she accepted gratefully, and asked him if he could come round. Now? He was ready for the request, eager to help this poor girl who had never known distress like this in her life before. Yet there was a selfish feeling inside him which made him glad: in her shock and discombobulation, she had asked to see him first.

When he arrived, she threw her arms around him, only stopping to explain to her children who this unknown man was – an old friend from a long time ago. Marika could never be told the truth, she felt, but noticed her daughter had a natural empathy with Shuo when he caressed her little head, which pleased her; it might even ease any explanation should it ever have to be divulged. But certainly not now.

She had to fly to London for the funeral but her children had not yet been given visas so were forced to stay behind: Shuo offered to do what he felt Berenice might ask him and help the maid to look after them while she was away, to which she readily agreed.

After she had departed, Shuo took them to a number of attractions to divert their attention from the loss of their father: he took some time off work and spent most of the weekend with them, always letting Berenice know where they were going and what they were doing.

For her, it was traumatic being in England alone at the funeral: although she knew many of her husband's work colleagues – and had worked with a few of them herself – she had never met his previous wife, Clarissa, whom she had not actually expected to turn up. Yet even she seemed shocked and distraught at what had happened and was very supportive, offering to help Berenice with the legal side if she wished it. Of Roger, there was no sign.

But Berenice did not wish for her help: she had heard from George how grasping the woman was and, even in her despair and sadness, decided to pay for all the legal advice she needed: George was rich – and she could afford to live in both China or England as she wished. The money would keep coming in for as long as his shows were being aired and franchised worldwide: his success and wealth would also mean she could buy outright the flat the TV company had provided for George, helped by the sale of her little flat, too. And she could visit their beloved Wiltshire house and London flat whenever she wanted: she had been blessed to meet him. How lucky she had been.

—∞—

When she returned to China and Shuo and her children greeted her at the airport, she realised once more how fortunate she had been to have Shuo to fall back on, reflecting on how she instinctively trusted him; he seemed to have made himself indispensable to her children while she had been away, too. On the way back to their flat in George's car, even the driver seemed subdued as the children regaled her with the things Shuo had taken them to see and do; and Marika in particular had an affinity with him that could not be denied. Yet Shuo was careful to ensure that their exuberance was not overdone: Berenice was still mourning for George and he whispered to the children that they must remember their father had just died and that Mummy was still sad as he cuddled them in the rear seat.

When they arrived back at her flat, Shuo discreetly departed to leave the family to themselves: he did not want to thrust himself on them and understood that they needed space to readjust: he was confident that Berenice would call him soon and that the children would expect her to anyway; and suddenly, he was happy once more, his torpor and lack of joy being banished as if like a warm sun after a hard winter.

Two days later, Berenice did indeed call him and asked if he would like to join the family for lunch at the weekend. He accepted willingly and cancelled a previous arrangement with a friend who had wanted to introduce him to a girl who might cheer him up. But with Berenice back in his life – however tenuously – he would now try for the greater prize...

The day came, and he found himself being in total harmony with the family, as if he were actually the master of the house and father to both children – rather than just the one – and husband to Berenice, too. His heart had surged at the emotion, but better was to come: in the evening, Xiao Jhong was being put to bed by the maid as Marika watched television and Berenice discreetly beckoned him into the privacy of the bedroom and asked him to sit on the bed as she walked agitatedly up and down.

The sun had dipped behind the horizon of tower blocks and the dimming light cast interrupted long shadows into the room and across the bed, like bars of a prison; yet Shuo sensed a feeling of impending freedom in Berenice's tone as she began to speak.

"Shuo, I want to thank you for being the true and loyal friend I always knew you to be, and for what you have done for my children – sorry, your and my children" – she gave him a sweet look – "and for helping me through this terrible time in my life." She paused, then stopped perambulating and looked him straight in the eye before saying: "I loved George deeply and he opened so many doors for me... he has left me one child, a beautiful house and a flat in England, lots of money, a job designing sets which I adore, and this beautiful flat here. He liberated me…"

Shuo's heart began to sink… was there a 'but' coming?

She turned and looked straight at him again, her beautiful eyes peering into his soul as if it was her trying to fathom him rather than Shuo wondering what she was going to say next.

"The point is," she continued, looking down at the floor and up to him as she spoke, as if unsure where to focus, "although we split up horribly and we both hated it, what happened actually turned out for the best. I don't mean George's dying," she added quickly, "but the fact he gave me everything I wanted. Yet… yet I often found myself thinking of you; as I say, George released me and gave me the strength to become a proper woman, which I now feel I am; he was a man, whereas I always felt you were still a boy."

Shuo went to protest, but she laid her forefinger on his lips. "Please, just let me speak for a little longer – I know you'll understand… Since our 'evening', I always knew that if something happened to George then I could rely on you, and the last two to three weeks have proved that. The children adore you and, to put it directly, so do I because you have become the man I thought you weren't before. So I'm asking if you would like to share my life here with me and help the children grow up, be my partner and grow old together."

Shuo was astonished: was he dreaming? And should he not be asking *her*? No – Berenice had to be in control and this was her way of proving it! All his hopes had been granted in a few short seconds and yet he could not believe she had said it. "Do you really mean that?" he asked warily, with a slight catch in his throat.

"Yes, I do, Shuo."

"Well… of course… yes! It would make me the happiest man in the world."

"Just one thing, though," she said, slightly sternly.

Ah, thought Shuo, *the caveat.*

"I don't want to marry again." Then in order to head off what she perceived would be a disappointment for him, she added, "Not you nor anyone. I have all I need now, emotionally, mentally and physically from the point of view of wealth, property and… well, you. I don't want to formalise our relationship – there's no need." She looked at him with her big, deeply enveloping brown eyes and he felt as if he was being drawn into those pools of mystery and just knew what the answer had to be.

"Yes, of course," he croaked.

"That's wonderful," she said, and was just about to throw her arms around him when the door burst open and Marika rushed in, with the maid in hot pursuit.

"Goodnight, Mummy," she said as she grasped her mother's leg. "I'm going to bed now."

"All right, darling," she said, and kissed her black hair with its little red bows and pigtails then knelt down to kiss her on the cheek. Then she said, looking at Shuo, "And kiss Daddy goodnight, too."

"Night night, Daddy," Marika said, kissing Shuo and then running out, as if it was the most normal thing in the world.

"You see?" said Berenice. "She loves you." And she lightly kissed Shuo, leaving him to his delighted disbelief as tears of happiness cascaded down his cheeks.

—m—

The days after that, Shuo gradually moved what important effects he had from his flat into Berenice's, and their lives became entwined like never before. He found a new energy and purpose in his work and soon became the manager at his company, turning it into a thriving and lucrative business. Yet, although he loved Berenice and had achieved what he feared would elude him, he could not help feeling on occasion that their relationship was as much business as pleasure: but that was Berenice's way. Always in control. And despite that, he loved it.

George had not loved his wife but had loved Berenice; Shuo had loved Berenice and thought he had loved Lin Yang but been subsumed by Berenice forever; Lin Yang had loved Shuo but the tensions with Berenice had caused her emotional imbalance and a senseless betrayal…

But the salient truth was that Berenice had floated serenely above them all, never having truly loved anyone in her life… at least not as much as she had ever loved herself.

Simon Holder

About the Author

—◆—

This is Simon Holder's second novel, [the first being an environmental thriller called The Revolution of the Species]. He has spent most of his life working in broadcast and corporate TV as a scriptwriter, producer and director at London Weekend Television, BBC West as a director/producer, creating documentaries, rock programmes, and items on pop, architecture, social issues and comedy; he then went freelance to work at an embryonic Sky TV, then made programmes for Channel 4, Central, Anglia, the BBC and many more. He has written a multitude of scripts for corporate and broadcast clients, including comedy and drama for the BBC and BT and also worked for a while at a TV company in Beijing, where much of the background material to this novel was culled. He was educated at Seaford College in Sussex and is passionate about the English language – in the late Bernard Levin's words, "one of the great contributions to the human race" – and is deeply concerned at its current demise. Simon's interests include classical music and opera – especially Berlioz and Porpora

– architecture, rugby union, The Strawbs, politics, theatre and cinema – and the protection of the British countryside. He lives in Wiltshire with his Chinese wife, Xiaomei, who helped immensely with the background intricacies of Chinese culture for this novel.